I0598441

ASHA HAWKINS

"Do I stand a chance?"

"God only knows, but you have a relationship with him, right? Ask, and you shall receive."

"She has great kick-boxing techniques and uses them to ground her opponents," Asha said.

"But you know how to defend against that. Concentrate."

"She also has a lot of power, as demonstrated with her knockout right hooks."

"You know how to defend against that, too. In fact, my dear Asha, you understand strategy and possess lightning speed yourself."

"Thanks for reminding me. But my strengths may be of no use against an android."

Also, by Scott Meehan

PRINCE OF BABYLON

STONE IN A SLING: A SOLDIER'S JOURNEY

DUTY RECALL

LOVE IN THE HOUSE OF WAR

FLAME IN PARADISE

MILLENNIAL GIRL

CROSSROADS

GIRL ALONE

QUANTUM ZONE: THUNDERBIRD

SILENCE IN HEAVEN

This book is a work of fiction. References to real people, events, establishments, organizations, or locales are intended only to provide a sense of authenticity and are used fictitiously. All characters, incidents, and dialogue, come from the authors imagination and are not to be interpreted as real. Any resemblance to actual persons, events, and entities is entirely coincidental.

DEDICATION

To the victims of human trafficking and the worlds oppressed.

"The Lord helps the fallen and lifts those bent beneath their loads" (Psalm 145:14).

Authors note

The future: Human trafficking grew into the largest illegal trade business, surpassing cocaine by 2020, and flourished by 2024. It was nothing that happened overnight, but a slow, festering growth, much like a virus or cancer in the world's societal culture against women.

The most significant driving force for this epidemic was the devastating wars place in Syria, Lebanon, Ukraine, Yemen, Iraq, Pakistan, Afghanistan, and throughout Africa, from 2014-2019. More than thirty-five million refugees fled the wars and persecution with millions of others internally displaced or forced to flee their homes.

With the revitalization of the Keystone pipeline under the new administration and the budget increase in the United States military, many Middle Eastern countries, such as Saudi Arabia, Turkey, and Iran assumed the slack that America left void when the government turned its attention inward. Several European nations like Russia, France, and Germany also stepped in to fill in the vacuum left by the United States that was becoming increasingly isolated than ever. Even Israel took on a new lead role as a world supplier of oil with their pipeline running through the Mediterranean to Greece and Italy, two major avenues into Europe. Great Britain also decided to focus more internally, resulting in a form of isolation like the United States.

Table of Contents

ONE - *Reflection*

March 2022 AD

I remember it all too well, a horrifying, vivid nightmare that was very real...and a traumatic moment I wish would simply go away forever.

"But it won't," Asha mumbled to herself. "I have to get through this."

Focusing back on the pages of her journal, she continued to read.

I was only two days away from completing my Special Forces training, the fifth and final phase. I was so close; I could taste the victory! It was in 202, the COVID year.

Asha raised her eyes briefly while running her tongue across her lips.

Just TWO DAYS AWAY, and I would become the first woman to ever be awarded the prestigious Green Beret!

Asha snuck a peek at the green felt beret placed neatly on her mantle and smiled.

I so wanted to follow in the footsteps of my father, Master Sergeant Ron Hawkins. He was a legend in his own right for his exploits in Afghanistan and Iraq. I would not even be here if he weren't so noble, rescuing a young Afghan girl in distress from the Taliban…She is my mother.

Asha sighed and looked up from her journal again, fixing her eyes on the portrait of her parents on her mantle. "Aah, come on, Ash, get through this tonight," she told herself in the mirror behind the portrait.

I was good at avoiding capture by the opposing force; in fact, I was good at everything I put my hands to throughout the training. Although my confidence soared, I knew in my heart that nothing is entirely predictable. However, I never in my wildest imagination would have believed that I would be betrayed...by my own team.

Asha started to close her journal again but kept her thumb inside the crease and forcibly opened it again. "Now, Ash, read it now!"

I cannot believe that I let my guard down, but I should have guessed by the comments made towards me that even these civilian volunteers who were supposed to be helping me were part of a good ole boy network...who dreaded the idea of a woman wearing the Green Beret.

When I followed my "team" into a dark, abandoned shack, a lantern suddenly flicked on, which was against our stealth protocol during the operation. This should have been my first clue that something was amiss.

Then, no less than five men surrounded me...none of whom looked at all friendly, including the ones who were on my team, the ones who led me here on false pretense. Don't show any fear, *I thought to myself.*

Before I could make for the door, one of them grabbed me by the arm while another lassoed me with a rope. I still had a free hand, a mistake for the nearest knucklehead. I reared back and let the dude who held my wrist have it just below his eye…I missed my target, which was the full flesh of his nose.

The hit was solid enough that it only angered him, and with the help from another punk, they succeeded in holding my hands behind my back. Too bad I was still half-tangled in the rope. Fortunately, I maintained some flexibility.

A toothy guy approached my front and said, "Time to teach you some manners, girly…uughh!"

That was all he was able to say because I didn't let him finish. Why should I have? I neither wanted to hear nor smell him. I swear, his breath reeked like he had been chewing skunk jerky or something. Foul wasn't the word for it. I wished I could have heaved on him.

But instead, with a grunt, I mustered my lower extremities with a full force of energy and placed a well-aimed kick right where it counts. "How's this for manners?" I yelled in the process.

"GAHH!" He doubled over, clutching his groin while screaming like a baby.

As for me, I was in full survival mode...my adrenaline running in high gear. The creeps behind me released their grip, either out of shock, fear, or both...and so I hoped.

Next, I went immediately into a basic shallow squat and waited. In hindsight, it would have been better if I had used this moment more wisely by running for the door. Unfortunately, I hesitated, only for a split second, but enough for it to become a costly mistake.

Because that's when I felt the most excruciating pain ever when the back of my leg gave way from a blunt, solid impact, just above my knee. The blow sent me crashing to the ground.

"Aaaahhhh! GOD!" I yelled. I remember that it really, really hurt…bad. I managed to turn quickly to see a giant buffoon standing over me with a baseball bat. He looked big and scary. Mud and sweat streaked his face, and his bare arms were muscular. He wasn't smiling. My skin twitched with alarm.

"Danger! Danger!" Asha blurted while throwing her journal across the room. Looking skyward, she uttered, "God…why? Why did this happen to me?"

Sliding her feet from under the covers, she stepped onto the carpet and hurried to the window. Breathing heavily, she threw it open to let the rush of cool air ride across her face. Asha's thick, dark hair tingled her shoulders and flowed in front of her like a waterfall when she leaned forward to pick up her journal.

Against the wall, Asha slid down at the window edge and allowed a teardrop to trickle down her cheek without wiping it away. Taking in the breeze and glimmering stars, she continued reading her journal.

Normally, I would have reacted with my lightning quick speed. However, that was now seriously hampered. Someone snuck up behind me out of nowhere and kicked me in the back. My momentum thrust me forward into the guy with the bat. So, the odds were five guys and a gorilla against one girl. This was not a pretty picture, to say the least.

Two of the men grabbed me from behind while I was eyeballing King Kong and tossed me against the back wall, away from the door. I hurt. For the first time that I could remember...I felt a deep sense of trepidation.

I tried to jump up, I really did, but when I stood on my right leg, I quickly went down again. I was a sitting duck. The next thing I knew, my body was taking punches from every angle…fists flying like I was a punching bag.

I tried my best just to cover my head and face while my arms, shoulders and back took the blows…at least at first. When I tried to protect my mid-section from savage kicking, I momentarily exposed my face, and like angry bees losing honey, they repeatedly stung my exposed flesh.

Just when everything started fading to black, I heard one of them yell, "That's enough, boys. I don't think she'll try kicking us again. Bill, Mike, tie her to the post."

I was too weak to resist the dirt bags from dragging me across the floor and then tying my hands above my head to a wooden beam or pole. I will never forget the amount of pain I was in…and I remember trying my best not to groan, because to me it was a sign of weakness.

Asha closed her eyes and looked skyward, taking a deep breath. Then she continued.

There I was, hanging with my arms extending above my head when the leader walked up to me and rubbed his nose on my bloodstained cheek. I could barely see out of my left eye, which was swollen shut. I remember being surprised that he wasn't the big goon. But this one had dark, evil eyes that pierced the soul.

"Quite a kick you have there, little darling. I betcha you can't do it again." He stepped back and nodded to the ape behind me, which I quickly surmised was the one holding the baseball bat, because he swung his blasted instrument of pain again, striking my other leg. I will never like the game of baseball again.

"Aaaahhhh—JESUS!" I yelled, panting for air like a hunted deer. I wanted to remain defiant, however...a bad habit of mine.

When I slurred, "You—your crazy swine!" through my gasping, I spit blood from my mouth like a stream from a kid's squirt gun, aiming right at him. I could not hide my smirk since the splat was a bullseye between those eyes.

The men standing around snickered. Dark eyes wiped the blood off with his sleeve and then reached around to grab the back of my hair. Yanking hard, he pulled my head close to his face. He tried to intimidate me by staring into my eyes while his nose was less than an inch from mine. I gave him the most defiant look that I could under the circumstances.

"I just saw something in your eyes that I didn't like, sweetie pie."

"Eh—twas the ref—reflection of the devil…you."

His piercing eyes continued to glare at me. "Wha—what doya want?"

"Want? You, of course. Just you—the first woman who is about to receive the Green Beret. You're special, and we want *a piece of you—especially the one you sent sprawling to the ground. Oh, he'll get up soon enough."*

"Gah—God beats thdevil."

"Well, darling, where is he now, hum?"

"Yu—yull see."

"Hear that, boys? Her God is going to get us," he mocked.

I winced when he placed his grubby hand on my cheek and left it there. I thought about taking a chomp into his wrist but didn't want to get rabies. Somewhere in the fracas, my hair came loose from the ponytail, and dirt-crusted, it was sticking to my face.

"I—I hate you. Don—don't touch me."

"You're quite a defiant little missy, aren't you?"

I was having more difficulty breathing as time went on, and I surmised that I was kicked or hit in the ribs. The muscles in my legs began to quiver also. Now I was worried that in a fleeting time shock would set in.

"Wa—water, ple—please."

The voice behind me yelled, "We—we should give her some water, Ray."

"Shut up, Jimmy!"

"Bu—but…"

"I said shut up! I know what I'm doing. Danny, grab me that bucket of water by the stool."

"Th—thanks," I murmured.

"You are quite welcome," he said, laughing as he threw water from the bucket into my face. "You see, darlin, in these high-stakes games, we must make it as real as we can. Unfortunately, people sometimes do tend to get hurt. We want you to be fully prepared for the real world…of a true Green Beret."

I closed my eyes, which were nearly shut anyway, because I could not stand the sight of him. Freako continued blabbing. "You're in our neck of the woods now, lil darlin. Have you ever heard the saying, 'What goes on in Vegas, stays in Vegas?'"

I forced my drooping head up a little and glared at my assailant, and with a meager grin I managed to say, "Nah—not Vegas, half-twit moron."

I know...not the brightest thing to say under the circumstances.

Instinctively, I tried to move my legs.

"Aaaahhhh...ma—ma legs! I think y— you broke them!"

"Such a pity, and so close to the end of selection, too. Guys, remove her boots."

While someone was busily removing my boots and socks...not gently, I might add, the ringleader grabbed my belt that was holding up my trousers, pulled out a large Buck knife, and cut it off. Then in one swift motion, he yanked my trousers down...over my throbbing legs.

"AAHH! GAAH!

I took a deep breath and whispered, "Hel—help me, Je—Jesus."

Then it happened...just when I thought bad would get very ugly, a blinding light appeared throughout the whole shack. I thought my prayer was answered and I was entering the gates of heaven. Then I heard the boisterous and life-saving sound of helicopter rotor blades.

The voice over the loudspeaker blared, "ALL CLEAR!"

The next thing I know, a bunch of soldiers burst into the shack. I barely saw them, but the first guy stopped and was pointing a .9mm pistol at the ringleader. "Get away from her, PUNK!" he snarled.

The leader nodded and backed away from me. One of the men behind me must have cut the rope because I dropped like a sack of potatoes with a thud. Somehow,

I stayed conscious, but barely. I only heard voices now...wanting just to go to sleep.

"Just following orders, sir."

Someone came over and covered me with a blanket or his shirt...or something. Thanks, I tried to say...but couldn't speak. He checked my vital signs, and I heard him say, "Captain, she's in a bad way."

The captain yelled, "Help him out. Secure a clearing to land the bird, now!"

The soldier helping me stood up, and I heard a commotion. Then I saw the ringleader fall beside me. He was bleeding profusely from his nose. Good, *I thought.*

Then I heard the captain again. "I will pull this trigger if you take another step! Now drop that bat, Sultan."

I heard that horrible thing drops to the ground next to me.

One of the bad guys said, "You can report us if you want, Captain, but we were ordered to treat her under the pretense of what she'd receive if captured for real by an actual hostile."

"Well, you bastards succeeded." The captain then spewed out a flow of words that would peel the paint off the wall.

Then I felt myself being scooped up by the soldier who came to my aid. He had me cradled with his massive arms up against his warm body. I remember trying to look at him but couldn't because of my head position. I was mumbling, "Dad? Dad?," but I was just dreaming. That was the last thing I remembered.

Asha closed her journal and rested her elbows on the windowsill. Looking up at the stars, she quoted a verse from the Psalms.

"Lord, your heavens declare your glory and night after night they reveal your knowledge. They have no speech; they use no words; no sound is heard

from them. Yet their voice goes out into all the earth, their words to the ends of the world."

TWO – *The Interview*

Asha was attractive, but not in the classic "Victoria's Secret" way. She was too strong and muscular for the lustrous look of a young catwalk model with glowing skin. She stood five feet, eight inches, and her smile was pleasantly reassuring without any measure of phoniness.

Yet in her serious nature, she was stunning—her eyes a deep, milk chocolate brown, tantalizing to anyone she stared at intently. A uniqueness radiated from within her to all genders. Men looked at her attentively, and women sought her friendship.

Asha sat confidently across from Captain Jacobs's metal gray-colored desk. She wore her army uniform and held a Green Beret deftly on her lap with both hands as if it were a sacred treasure.

It had been four months since her ordeal during Phase V. Four of six local Carolinian men were convicted of assault with a deadly weapon and attempted rape. One of the two not convicted received a misdemeanor for testifying about the whole episode. The other man was not charged since he spent his time on the ground throughout the incident after being kicked by Asha. Although he attempted to sue her for injury, his case was dismissed.

Jacobs awkwardly failed in his attempts to appear more focused on the file lying in front of him than at her penetrating, almond-shaped, brown eyes.

"I know your father, Master Sergeant Ron Hawkins—how is he doing?"

Asha watched the twenty-eight-year-old commander and took mental notes whenever his round pale blue eyes engaged hers. "He is doing well, sir, and is as strong as ever. Thank you for asking," she answered with a grateful smile. "How well do you know him?"

"I met him a couple of times before he retired. I was a young Lieutenant. He smiled often and offered his help on many occasions."

"That sounds like him."

"But about you. I see some of him in you. I am impressed with your martial arts skills, as well as your multi-language skills."

"Thank you, sir."

"You obtained your black belt in karate before you graduated high school?"

"Yes, sir, I was the state champion for the sixteen to seventeen-year-old age group in Tennessee."

Jacobs regarded her admirably and allowed a slight smile. "Congratulations."

"My parents instilled a sense of fearlessness in me when I was a young girl. They were inspirational to me in so many ways, including my strong commitment to God and family."

Jacobs nodded his head. "Your record at the academy is most impressive. You entered after graduating top of your class at Clarksville Academy in 2020 and had the opportunity to attend the Naval and Air Force Academy, and West Point? Why did you choose to enlist in the National Guard?"

Asha felt it natural to follow in the footsteps of her father to choose enlistment rather than being an officer. Her father tried to discourage her, but in the end he supported her final decision. I felt a special obligation to be a soldier. And the world needs people like me now, not four years from now. My greatest hero in the world is my father. I wanted to be just like him as a soldier."

"He wanted you to be enlisted?"

"He would have been delighted if I had selected any of the academies."

"Where did you learn your mastery of foreign languages?"

"My mother is fluent in Farsi, Pashto, and Russian. Picking up Arabic from my adopted sister seemed natural."

"Wow! So, you know four other languages?"

"A total of seven, including English. I speak Spanish, German, and French. I do not know the Orient languages like Chinese yet."

"Yet?" They both laughed.

"Your adopted sister, Mariam, she's the one your father rescued from ISIS back in 2014?"

"Yes, sir. You are familiar with the mission?"

"One for the books." Jacobs scanned the portfolio further. "You majored in pre-med studies with a specialty in Advanced Medical Cybernetic Technologies." His commanding voice reflected his approbation towards his latest candidate.

Asha's dream was to become an elite member of his Special Forces Operational Detachment Alpha (ODA), team. "Yes, sir."

"Tell me a little about your medical specialty."

Asha leaned forward and spoke with confidence. "I was involved with clinical cytogenetic research that concentrated on the latest integration technologies between humanoid-cyborg and human-space technology. This included medical studies in the advancements made in state-of-the-art androids."

Captain Jacobs looked at her with astonishment. "And despite all your accomplishments, you decided to rock the boat.

"Sir?"

"You turned down all the plush assignments in D.C.—a career at the Pentagon."

"Yes, sir."

"Just to volunteer for the Special Forces Qualification course at Bragg?"

Asha did not hesitate. "Yes, sir!"

"And you knew that no other female had ever succeeded in finishing the full course?"

"Yes, sir, I knew."

"And here you are—the first female to obtain the Green Beret."

"Yes, sir, although I admit that it was a grueling process, except for the timed, long-distance day and night land navigation course. That was fun."

"Let me guess. Your father took you camping when you were growing up."

Asha chuckled. "Yes, sir, along with my brothers. And I might add, we had to carry heavy loads, in adverse weather, and in rough, hilly terrain."

Jacobs laughed. "I bet you did."

"Did you know that your Language Aptitude Test of 145 was off the charts?"

"Not at that time, sir."

"In fact, it was the highest score ever recorded."

"That's what I've been told, sir."

Jacobs looked at her for a moment. "One more thing. Your Phase V experience. I want to make sure that it is completely behind you."

Asha fidgeted, the first sign of diminished confidence she had held throughout the interview. *I knew this would come up,* she thought.

"I remember telling my family, 'Only four more weeks,'" she answered, trying to move past the worse part.

"But it was those last four weeks that almost led to your complete downfall. Are you over those events?"

"I believe I am, sir, yes."

"You don't seem so sure. Why don't you tell me what happened…in your words?"

"Do I have to, sir—I mean, talk about that again?"

Jacobs nodded his head.

"But why?"

"Sergeant Hawkins. As a team facing the life-and-death dynamics that we do at any given moment, I need to be sure that you have nothing inhibiting your mental and emotional state."

Asha nodded her head. "Well, sir, on the third night of the fourth and final week, I led a small team on an ambush operation in a remote location. My plan looked solid, and the cadre approved it. But before the raid commenced, my team told me about an OPFOR prisoner they were holding at an abandoned shack. They told me he had great intelligence. Turned out to be a set-up."

"Why did they turn on you?"

"I don't know why, but one of them suddenly hit me with a baseball bat."

"They claimed it was self-defense."

Asha looked abandoned as she continued. "It was me who attempted self-defense, sir…but sadly, I was outnumbered."

"But you were able to kick one of them."

"Yes, sir, I did. After that was when I was hit with the bat."

"So, you struck the first blow, the reason why they claimed self-defense."

Asha's pleasantries vanished, and she answered the captain tersely. "Do you believe that…SIR?"

Jacobs eyes squinted. "No, Sergeant Hawkins. I do not believe they acted in self-defense. In the end, you were awarded the Green Beret."

"A panel decided that I would have made it if not for the assault…in fact, I had racked up enough points from the previous phases."

"What about you?"

"Sir?"

"Do you think that you deserved the Green Beret?"

Asha kneaded the beret in her hands and looked at it. Then she looked up at him and stood slowly. "I am sorry to have wasted your time, sir."

Jacobs responded, "Wait! Sit down—please. I just wanted to make sure that you honestly felt that you earned it…because you did."

Asha complied.

"I apologize for the way I asked you."

Asha nodded her head.

"How did you come about this interview today?"

She thought a moment. "I received an official letter delivered to my home, sir."

"But you don't know who sent it?"

Looking at Jacobs, she answered, "The Department of Defense."

"Well, we just use their letterhead. I'll tell you…it was me."

"You, Captain Jacobs?"

"That's right. You see, it was me who barged into the shack and rescued you from those scum."

Asha stared at him in disbelief.

"You wouldn't have remembered because you were out cold. But the bottom line is that I requested this interview because I want you on my team—if you still want to be on it."

Asha looking confused, regained her composure, stood up and reached for his hand. "Yes, sir! Thank you, sir! I—I don't know what to say, but yes! I'm thrilled!"

Jacobs smiled. "Believe me, we are thrilled as well. The big guy who picked you up—he's our senior NCO and will see to your needs."

"That's—that's so awesome, sir! Thank you so much!"

"Why don't you go on home for the day, and we'll see you early tomorrow morning to begin training. You'll jump right in with the guys."

Closing her eyes, she punched the sky and blurted, "YESSS—I'm on the team!"

Captain Jacobs stood with a smile. "Welcome to the team, Sergeant Hawkins!"

Asha moved towards him to give him a hug but stopped abruptly, much to his disappointment, and held out her hand. "Thank you again, sir! You will not be disappointed!"

Jacobs took her hand and said, "I'm sure of it."

Before she cleared the doorway, Captain Jacobs yelled, "Oh, and we have you scheduled for HALO school next month."

Asha peeked around the corner and gave him a wide-eyed look. "YESSS!"

THREE - Kidnapped

Fourteen-year-old Nicole Anderson sprinted down the stairs. Her sand-colored, sleek, straight hair flowed behind her like wings until she stopped at the bottom.

Ethan and Levi were too busy playing the new NBA 3k25 video game on the family's large 65-inch Smart TV to pay much attention to her dress. Just what she was hoping.

"I'll be home for dinner," Nicole called to them. Engrossed in their intense competition, one yelled back, "Okay!"

Closing the door behind her, she glanced at her watch. Nicole wore a bright colored, patterned autumn dress and a pair of shaker bow flat shoes to reach her destination. Leaving her five-bedroom, two-story home on Birnam Wood Drive, she walked towards the corner of Old Falls and Swinks Mill Road, which was a quarter mile away.

When she arrived at the circle, she watched the cars go by while restraining the breeze-lifting skirt that hung two inches above her knees.

Ten minutes later, a shiny black sports sedan pulled up to the curb and a handsome man sporting a pair of mirror sunglasses poked his head out the window. With a charming smile, he said, "Hey gorgeous, there you are. Get in, hurry."

Nicole did a double take before sliding into the passenger seat. "Wow, Chad, where did you get this car? It looks brand new!"

"It is new; a 2025 Saab. I am extremely glad to see you."

"Well, don't forget, I need to be home before five," she added while surveying the plush interior.

"You won't have to worry about that, baby. Here, I have something for you."

The manner of his reply escaped her attention. "What is it?"

"Some brew I made. It's good."

Nicole hesitated but allowed herself to drink from the cup that Chad handed her. After making a peculiar face, she added, "It's a little sweet but not too bad."

"It takes a little getting used to."

Nicole had met Chad several days before when he approached her at a popular coffee shop. Showering her with a wave of praise, he told the cashier, "I'm paying for whatever this pretty girl wants."

Startled by such charm and random generosity, Nicole turned to see a dashing young man smiling at her. When he invited her to sit with him, she hesitated before complying. By the time they finished their Frappuccino's, he had asked her out on a date.

"But I'm only fourteen!" she exclaimed, hoping not to scare him off.

"What? No way! You look at least sixteen, and besides, I'm seventeen."

"Really? You look like you're, um, twenty?"

"Twenty?" Chad chuckled. "Wow. Everybody keeps telling me this, but it's not true."

Nicole laughed nervously. "I'm sorry. I didn't mean to…"

"Don't be. It's okay. Besides, nobody will think anything about us being together. We look close enough to be the same age."

"But I don't even know you."

"You'll give me some time to get acquainted. I attend McLean High," he lied, "so I'm—around."

"Well, I suppose we could go on a short date, but I'd have to ask my mom first."

"Aw, come on. We would just meet for coffee or something after school…like we're doing now. Your mom would just think we were friends from school or something—hanging out."

Nicole still seemed a bit tentative. "Well, I am almost fifteen. Okay, just a coffee, and then you would bring me back home before dinner?"

"Yes, of course, if that's all you want. I'm a patient guy; I just want to be with you."

"Alright. I'll meet you on Friday. My mom arrives home later on Fridays. Should I meet you here?"

"No, I have a better place in mind. I can pick you up at the little square where Old Falls and Swinks Mill connect at, say, three-thirty?"

"Yes, I know where that is. I live less than a mile from there."

"Great, see you there, and don't worry, I'll have you back home by five."

"Okay, Chad. See you then," Nicole said with a wide smile.

"Whatshin disss dree?" Nicole began but could not finish before dropping the cup on her lap, slumping back against the passenger door.

"Aww, you stupid…" A horn blast caused Chad to swerve away from an oncoming car when he tried to catch the cup containing the liquid—a Sprite mixed with gamma hydroxybutyric acid—the colorless, odorless liquid used to knock out unsuspecting victims.

W

A dozen or so people, all veterans, attended the small conference at the White House, along with the President of the United States and a couple of members of his staff. Caterers served coffee and pastries throughout the gathering. The topic of the morning was a brainstorming session for the upcoming National Memorial Day Observance at Arlington National Cemetery.

As the meeting convened and the chatter continued down the hall towards the exit, the president moved to the Oval Office, taking a seat in his leather chair. Two staff members and two Secret Service bodyguards occupied the room. One of them appeared visibly upset.

"Bob?"

Robert Anderson hurried towards the president. "Yes, Mr. President?"

The president stopped signing documents and glanced up at his most trusted bodyguard standing over him. "What's wrong? Something is troubling you. You're not yourself."

Bob hesitated before stuttering, "Its-its Nicole, sir. She's…"

"What is it, Bob?"

"Well, sir, she's missing. She did not come home last night. Lorrie and I have frantically questioned all of her friends, teachers, everybody we could think of, and…" His voice trailed off in a quiver.

"Everybody, clear the room—now!" the president announced as he stood up to place his arm around Bob's shoulder.

Those present exited his office without hesitation.

"Bob, come on and sit down." The president led him towards the leather couch.

"It's just not like her," Bob sobbed.

"I know, Bob, I know."

"She-she…" Bob couldn't finish.

The president had never seen Robert Anderson, ex-Navy SEAL, retired commander, act so helpless.

"Where's Lorrie now?"

"She's been with the police all day. Her parents are on the way here from New York. She's—she's a wreck. So, am I, for that matter?"

"Bob, go home. Take care of this, and do not come back here until this is resolved."

Bob looked at him, trying to hide the tears by wiping his eyes. "Sir, you rely on me to protect you. You…"

The president didn't let him finish. "Now, Bob! That is an order. You need to be home. Moran will have a replacement."

Bob opened his mouth but did not respond. He nodded his head and got up from the couch. "Tha—thank you, sir."

"Bob."

He turned slowly and looked at the powerful man he swore to protect. "Mr. President?"

"We will get Nicole back, no matter the cost. I will personally see to it! I promise. Do you understand?"

He nodded his head again as he departed the Oval Office.

All day, the President couldn't concentrate on anything except for his Secret Service agent's dilemma. He'd contacted the head of the Secret Service, Ken Moran, to arrange backup. "He and the whole family must be going through hell," the president said to Ken.

"Yes, sir. We will give him all the support he needs, and then some. Our agency will not rest until Nicole is found."

"I'm sure he is torn between duty to the president and his family. He needs to be home with them at a time like this."

"Yes, sir, I agree. He wouldn't be of any service to you in his present state of mind."

Later that night in the dark bedroom on the second floor in the southwest corner of the White House, the president tossed and turned. His sleeplessness caused the First Lady to wake.

"It's Bob and Lorrie, isn't it?" she asked.

The president had two daughters of his own and was troubled. "That could have been one of ours, you know."

"No, it could not have. They are too well-protected."

"You know what I mean. This is too close to home!"

"Well, honey. Let me remind you of something. You are the President of the United States of America."

"So?"

"So, what arc you going to do about it?"

"That's what I've been racking my brain about all day and night. I don't want to jeopardize Nicole's life. Those responsible have no idea who they have."

"Let's hope this is true; otherwise, it could be a planned operation involving a ransom."

"Our people are tracking that angle, but nobody has contacted the Andersons. I tend to think more like what our Homeland Director briefed us on earlier, about the human trafficking cartels increasing their efforts here in the U.S. These people are powerful."

"And so are you!"

The POTUS looked over at his wife. "You're right, of course...by God, they cannot get away with this."

The First Lady leaned over and turned on the light switch, then sat up. "Do you remember the award ceremony you attended at Fort Bragg three months ago?"

The president thought for a moment. "I attend a lot of them. Which one?"

"The one where you pinned a medal on the first female recipient of the Green Beret."

"Yes, Sergeant Hawkins. What about her?"

"Well, besides telling her how proud you were of her, you told her how much you looked forward to the time when she could be of service to you and our nation."

The president smiled. "You're right! Sergeant Hawkins. Asha Hawkins, if I recall correctly. Her dad is a retired Green

Beret, and her mom is from Afghanistan. I remember her story."

"Well, Mr. President, she may be just what you need for this mission."

Without saying another word, he swung his pajama-covered legs out of bed and walked towards the phone.

"Who are you calling at three in the morning?" she asked while glancing at her watch.

"Anybody I damn well please!" he retorted.

The First Lady chuckled. "You go, Mr. President! I'm going back to sleep."

The duty officer snatched up the red-lit phone. "Yes, Mr. President!"

"Get me General Sheffield!"

There were no questions asked or reminders of the time, just the sharp voice from an army major. "Yes, sir, Mr. President!" He played with the computer in front of him with rapid determination and found Sergeant General Sheffield's number in seconds. Without hesitation, he placed the call through and waited for the connection. A dazed voice answered.

"I have the president on the line, sir." As the major transferred the call, Sergeant General Sheffield fumbled for his glasses and the light switch, waking up his wife in the process. She heard his stern voice.

"Yes, Mr. President, I'm awake. No, no, sir, no trouble at all." His wife muffled her attempt to laugh. "Yes, sir. Nine o'clock in the West Wing. Yes, sir, I'll be there. Yes, goodnight, sir."

"What was that all about?" his wife asked indigently.

"I'm not sure," General Sheffield answered as he got out of bed and strolled downstairs to the kitchen for coffee. He turned on the news channels to search for any clues. He couldn't find anything on the news beyond the basic nonsense, yet he continued to drink coffee, channel surf, and remain awake, wondering and worrying about the meeting scheduled six hours away.

FOUR – Human Trafficking

A Secret Service member led General Sheffield into the Oval Office ten minutes before the scheduled meeting time. It wasn't the first time he laid eyes on the large antique desk, draped flags, and the seal of the republic, but he made eye contact with each item, nonetheless. Another man the general recognized as Ken Perkins was already in the room, still standing, as if waiting for the general's arrival.

Despite getting little sleep, a hot shower and breakfast before the meeting, the president was in an abysmal mood. He asked both men to take a seat on the couch while he moved from behind the desk to a single armchair across from them.

Looking at Ken, the president began. "Human trafficking?! I want more! I want everything you have on it—on this so-called current trend you mentioned a couple of weeks ago."

"Current trend, sir?"

"Yes, why it's hit our country hard in the past couple of months. In fact, I just received word this morning that there were five girls missing in the past twenty-four hours here in D.C. and in Baltimore alone. This cannot be a coincidence, can it, Ken?"

"Ah, no, sir. I'll have a report for you, everything you want to know. Forty-eight hours, Mr. President?"

The president stood up, held his outstretched hand towards the DOHS Chief, and led him towards the door.

"I appreciate your hard work, Mr. Perkins. You have twenty-four hours," he answered with a smile as a Secret Service member ushered him the rest of the way out of the Oval Office. "Oh, and be sure to get me some information on this business with cyborgs."

"Cyborgs, sir?"

"Yes, you know, robots, androids, synthetics, whatever you want to call them now. Establish a connection between robots and human trafficking."

"Yes, Mr. President, I'm on it."

The president sat down again, as did the general, who looked confused. His attention now focused on the general, the president uttered, "Sergeant Asha Hawkins."

"Sir?"

"I need her, General. I need her now. I also need all the files you have on her, West Point evaluations, her role within a Special Ops A-Team, everything."

"She did not attend West Point, sir."

"I thought she was accepted."

"She was. But she turned them down to attend the Special Forces training from her Guard unit."

"Oh wow. I did not know."

Do you still want her? She does have a Top-Secret file already."

"Yes. And give me everything on her. Everything. I'm aware of her implanted biotechnical assets during the operation."

The general cracked a slight smile. "Twenty-four hours, Mr. President?"

"ASAP, General. You have four hours for her record." He paused. "But I'll give you the twenty-four to have her here in my office."

General Sheffield's grin vanished. "Yes, sir, I'll get right on it!"

The commander in chief stood up and for the second time extended his hand while walking towards the door. "I know you will, General Sheffield. I can always count on you," the president answered, grinning from ear-to-ear.

The longhaired brunette screamed above the roar, "GO, SETH!"

Caleb and Miriam sat on either side of her, Miriam covering her ears. Asha loved her adopted sister as much as her two brothers, but tonight was Seth's night, his first NHL game with the Nashville Predators.

She didn't hear her mobile phone ring because of the noise, but the vibration on her smart watch alerted her to an incoming call.

The name on the screen flashed, *Captain Jacobs*. "Oh great!" Asha muttered in aggravation. She tapped Caleb on the shoulder. "Excuse me; I need to take a phone call."

"What?" Caleb exclaimed. "Seth's on the ice now!"

"Right! Okay, once his shift changes, I have to run!"

Caleb gave her an appalled look and shook his head.

Asha looked troubled. "I'm sorry. It was my boss."

Once Seth skated towards the bench, Asha squeezed through a couple of fans, carefully stepping around protruding legs, and avoiding any eye contact with disrupted fans. Heading through the exit and into the arena's concession and souvenir area, she found a semi-quiet spot to speed-dial her boss. "Sir, I just got your call."

"Hello, Asha. Where are you?"

"At the Predators game...in Nashville. What's up?"

"Can't say over the phone. Can you come by the office tonight?"

"Tonight? Sir, you know I've only been back from the last mission less than a month. I'm supposed to get…"

"Some down time, I know, I know. This is urgent, or I wouldn't be calling you."

"Yes, sir. Okay, I'm leaving now."

"Thanks, Asha. I wish I could say finish the game, but I'll see you when you get here…oh, your brother. How's he doing?"

"He's holding his own and getting his fair share of minutes."

"They're playing the Dallas Stars, aren't they?"

"Yes."

"Who's winning?"

"We are, 1-0!"

"You're assuming I'm a Predators fan?"

"You mean you aren't?"

Jacobs laughed. "Of course. Just messing with you. Drive safely."

Two hours later, Sergeant Hawkins entered Captain Jacob's office, the only room in the building with a light still on.

"Sir, where is everybody? I'm the first one here?"

"Sit down, Asha. You're the only one here, besides me of course. I'm not expecting anyone else."

"What—what's going on, sir?"

Captain Jacobs grinned. "You're not going to believe this. Colonel Crowell called me and said that the Joint Chairman, Sergeant General Sheffield, called him, giving the order to have you on the next available flight to Washington."

"What? Why am I going to Washington?"

"To see the president!"

"Yeah, right."

"I'm serious."

"Does this have something to do with my last mission in Bangladesh?"

"I don't think so. The JCOS told the colonel if there were no available flights in the morning to have you on a chartered private aircraft. He wants you there by tomorrow."

"That's crazy!"

"Well, the colonel said the general wasn't telling him anything except to say that this was no ceremony and for you to leave your uniform at home."

"Wha…?"

"I don't know. Anyway, here is your ticket. You leave Nashville at nine in the morning, and someone will pick you up at the airport."

"Great."

"Don't worry. You'll arrive at 1300 hours, plenty of time to be taken to your hotel to get prepped for your meeting with the POTUS."

"What time is my meeting?"

"They want you at the White House by 1600."

"Somebody will pick me up. Couldn't I just rent a new XL-Proxima?"

"Ha! No way, Asha."

"But sir, come on."

"Nope. Cannot have the president see a girl riding up in a speed-racer motorbike. He'll begin to wonder about our budget requests."

Asha looked over her ticket and then backed up at Captain Jacobs. "Will that be all, sir?"

Jacobs looked back at her without a smile. "Yes and be careful. I don't know what this is all about, but if the president wants to see you in his office, it's going to be very sticky."

"You and the team will be the first to know if he has any plans for us."

Captain Jacobs shook his head. "Goodnight, Asha. Get some sleep. I have a feeling you're going to need it."

Asha stood up. "Goodnight, sir."

"I mean it! Get some rest!"

"Not to worry. I'm used to keeping my lamp burning."

"Huh?"

"Goodnight, sir."

The flight from Nashville to Reagan National was uneventful. Asha traveled light and intended to grab her small suitcase off the conveyer belt but was confronted by a well-dressed female agent. "Asha Hawkins," she stated firmly, "please follow me."

"But I have a bag at..." She didn't finish.

"All taken care of, ma'am."

Asha followed the agent to a shiny black Saab sports sedan waiting for her. Before sliding into the plush leather seats in the back, she noticed a male agent place her suitcase into the trunk. Placing her hand on the seat, she mumbled,

"Wow, Jake, you sure know how to make up for not having a Proxima!"

The vehicle merged into traffic and headed to her hotel in Crystal City. Stopping in front of the hotel, the agent led her straight away to her room. "Go ahead and get settled. We took the liberty to pick up some items that you'll find in the closet. We'll be around if you need us."

Asha watched the agent leave. "Okay, thank you."

Walking to the closet first, she swung open the doors. Hanging from the wooden rod was a tan Tahari jacket and charcoal skirt suited for the special occasion. "Hmm, the president's taste isn't bad at all," she whispered.

Below the clothes on the floor were a pair of black ankle-strap dress sandals, the latest in Steve Maddens shoe collection. "Okay, then. All set. I'll just take my shower now."

Asha kept her voice low as if she were dictating notes to herself but didn't want anyone else to hear. Walking to the stylish bathroom, Asha checked everything before turning on the hot water from the shower. As she began to undress from her travel clothes, she added, "Now what could the POTUS want with little ole me?"

The president was wrapping up a long day and looked forward to his next meeting. The file for Sergeant Hawkins was as thick as the normal military files on generals, which was what he was used to previewing before selecting a chairman.

The front page held a summary of her duty stations, job titles, schools, and other basic information all condensed on her Officer Record Brief, abbreviated as ORB. There was a full-length photo of

Asha in her Dress Blue uniform. The president studied the photo a few seconds.

There was a separate file marked "Top Secret" that held his specific focus. "Yes, I believe she'll fill the role quite well," he muttered to himself.

The photo portrayed her five-foot, eight-inch frame, deep brown eyes, and dark chestnut hair, in a ponytail. Her smile exhibited full confidence yet was eye-catching.

The president took forty minutes looking through her portfolio after Sergeant General Sheffield delivered it himself. Earlier that morning, when he handed the packet over to the president's secretary, the general was promptly, but respectfully, dismissed. "The president would like to review her profile in solitude. This way, he can generate his questions and comments without any external influence. His method, of course."

"Of course," General Sheffield replied. "Should I wait around here or go back to the Pentagon?"

"He'll contact you when he's ready."

General Sheffield nodded, then turned around to leave. "He knows where to find me. Oh, could you let him know that Sergeant Hawkins will arrive at 1:00 pm today?"

"I will let him know, General. Thank you."

FIVE – Human Trafficking Stats

Dear Mr. President,

I have the honor to present the report on the human trafficking dilemma.

ABSTRACT - Human trafficking has exploded into a $100-billion global industry, with sexual trafficking constituting the majority. Profits from sexual trafficking are estimated to be as high as $40 billion annually. As many as 40,000 people are trafficked into the United States every year for the purposes of forced labor and sexual exploitation. The profiteer remains a threat to their victims and to anyone endeavoring to rescue them.

ORIGINS: Greeks were famous for carting off young women after battles. The human booty was consigned to lives of servitude, either as concubines or domestic servants. In Rome, at the height of its empire, one in every three people is thought to have been a slave. Enslaved men toiled as laborers; girls and women channeled into entertainment avenues.

RECENT HISTORY: Since 2000, prostitution scandals involving U.N. peacekeeping troops and defense contractors have increased dramatically. In Liberia, U.N. administrators were implicated in a fraud where food aid was used to force girls and women into servicing peacekeeping troops and local executives.

In 2002, an employee of DynCorp Corp. testified to Congress that fellow workers in Bosnia had bought girls to keep in their homes as sex slaves. Regardless, the company went on to receive a no-bid contract the following year to provide law enforcement and prison operations in post-conflict Iraq.

GEOGRAPHY: 70 million people worldwide are victims of modern-day slavery. Although the sex industry affects every continent, it is estimated that 500,000 southeast and south-central Asian girls are believed to be working in the sex industry in India, Ukraine, and most recently Dubai. Other locations on the rise include Colombia, Brazil, Venezuela, and Ecuador.

VICTIMS: The international commercial sex trade exploits six million children. Ninety percent of those sold into sexual slavery are under twenty-four, and some are as young as six years old. Ninety percent of the women and girls between the ages of 15-30 take steroids to make themselves more attractive to clients, but the side effects are devastating. Eighty percent of the prostituted women enter sexual slavery before age 18.

PROFITS: More than $100 billion in profits are generated annually by the human trafficking industry. Although several major cartels exist across the globe, Smith Robotics, Inc., is said to generate the largest revenue, profits that derive from a combination of the latest cyber technology and the largest employment of female employees, officially labeled as displaced refugees.

STRUCTURES: 80,000 children in failed states have been left without either parent due to adult migration. Organized crime networks control 99 percent of prostituted women throughout Europe, the Middle East, and Asia. Smith Robotics, Inc., receives financial backing from scientific institutions, government agencies, and educational departments for scientific research.

CHALLENGES: Due to the tremendous number of profits involved, there are multiple handlers between initial contact with the victim and the end-state controller. It is extremely difficult to bring legal charges against the chief financiers and government officials involved at prominent levels. Personal armies and the latest technological cyborgs protect Smith Robotics, Inc., from outside interference, and it has been reported that extreme violence is used as a deterrent against any entity challenging his realm.

CONSEQUENCES: Human trafficking has grown to the largest cartel-led unlawful criminal activity in the world. Its effects cause disastrous societal damage that spreads to violence, disease, broken relationships, and broken human spirits.

SUMMATION: Human trafficking has become an uncontrollable worldwide pandemic operated by some of the wealthiest and most powerful people across the globe. Intelligence reports that many victims have been taken through a precise, high-tech selection process for cyborg experimentation and in preparation for future trips to Mars colonies.

KEN PERKINS

Ken Perkins

Secretary of Homeland Security

Department of Homeland Security (DHS)

SIX – Meeting the President

The president finished reading the DHS report on human trafficking just prior to his phone lighting up.

"Sergeant Hawkins is here, sir," his secretary said with anticipation.

"Send her in."

Seconds later, a bodyguard opened the door to the Oval Office and led Asha inside. "Sergeant Hawkins, sir."

The president responded along with a wave of the hand, "Thanks, Jeff."

The Secret Service agent nodded and shut the door behind him.

The president walked towards Asha with his right hand extended. "Good to see you again, Sergeant Hawkins. Thanks for coming."

Taking his hand, she replied with a smile, "Likewise, Mr. President, my pleasure!"

The president held on to her hand before leading her towards the couch. "Please have a seat and make yourself comfortable."

"Thank you, sir."

"Can I get you anything? Water? Coffee?"

"No, sir, I'm fine, thank you."

The president went to the mini-refrigerator and grabbed two bottles of water. Holding one of them up, he added, "Are you sure? They have the Presidential Seal."

Asha chuckled. "Well, okay, Mr. President, thank you."

After handing her a bottle of water wrapped in a napkin, the president sat across from her in the armchair.

"How are your parents?"

"They're doing well, sir, thanks for asking."

"They're in India, aren't they—doing missions work?"

"Yes, sir, they're working with Project Rescue, an organization committed to rescuing and restoring girl victims of sex trafficking worldwide."

"Yes, quite interesting. You just completed a mission in Bangladesh involving human trafficking."

"Yes, sir, less than a month ago."

"I read the report. Magnificent work, you, and your team."

"Thank you, sir."

"You may have heard, but here in this area alone we just had five teenage girl disappearances in the past three days."

"No, sir, I was not aware!" Asha answered.

"Yes, in fact, one of the fourteen-year-old girls is the daughter of my personal bodyguard.

"My God, sir, I'm sorry."

"Her name is Nicole. The fact is, we, some of our agency heads, have considerable information on those responsible, those behind this operational network."

"You do, sir?" Asha leaned forward. "Is there anything we can do?"

The president smiled, realizing this conversation was going down the path he wanted it to go. "There is no 'we', Sergeant Hawkins. Just you."

"Sir?"

"The reason I summoned you here alone."

Asha tried to hide her dismay. "It is? You mean my team won't be joining me?"

The president studied the strong-willed American Special Forces soldier that the media had dubbed *The Millennial Girl.* "That's correct. I have a mission for you, but your team will not be involved."

She responded with a look of wonderment, and though her lips moved, she didn't utter a sound in response.

"This bothers you, Sergeant Hawkins?" the president asked, using her rank.

Asha was quick to respond. "Oh no, sir, Mr. President. Not at all. I may have been…"

"A little surprised?"

"Yes, sir, surprised is a good word." Sitting up straight, Asha continued. "Sir, I would be honored to fulfill any mission you've selected for me to accomplish. I can do it...I will do it!"

The president refrained from showing his extreme pleasure. "Excellent! I've arranged with the chairman, General Sheffield, to transfer all your records here for an assignment to the White House.

You'll receive your orders before the end of the day."

Waiting for the president to pause, Asha asked, "May I ask what my mission is, sir?"

"You've heard of the Jedburghs?"

"Yes, sir, the Jeds, as we referred to them. We studied them at the academy and while I was going through the Special Forces training. They began in 1944 during World War II."

"So, you're familiar with their operations. Good."

"Yes, Mr. President, in fact, we've been following their pattern during our team training."

"I'm glad to hear that, Sergeant Hawkins, because this was something I've always wanted to implement down to our frontline teams. Oh, I've met with the usual resistance from the conventional types, however."

"Yes, sir, we—at least our group, have been training with three-person teams. The training process involves coordinated attacks with Indigenous people."

"So, how is that going? I mean, is the Special Forces community behind this idea?"

"Well, sir, since we train in the science of social movements and terrorism, as well as different languages, political theory, and the historical culture of specific regions, we're definitely engaged with the program," she answered as if she'd been reading from a brochure.

"Good. I'll take that as a positive. Sounds like your unit is tracking. I ask because for this mission, I want you to assemble a three-woman team, modeled after the 'Jeds'. Now, before you say anything, I know you're the only female Special Forces operative now."

"Yes, sir."

"You—the three of you, will study the operation of a high-tech cartel, led by a multi-billionaire, Stan Smith. Ever hear of him?"

"Yes, sir, I've heard of him, but he's never been on our radar for any reason."

"Until now!" the president answered.

"Do you believe he's behind this latest kidnapping?"

"Yes, I do. And I need you to find out where they've taken Nicole and the other four missing girls and bring them home.

"Yes, sir."

"Your secondary mission is to destroy Smith's cyber-human trafficking network, which is responsible for this. His operation has gotten out of control."

Asha's eyes widened with excitement, but she held her tongue for the moment.

"Now, I'll allow you to select two others at your discretion. I'll provide you with a couple of potential members, and of course, you can have complete access to their files." The president leaned forward. "This will be a very challenging mission, Sergeant Hawkins, but I believe you're up to the task."

"Yes, sir, I am. I am not afraid, and I serve a mighty God who has seen me through thick and thin."

The president glared at her. "That's what I thought about you, your gallantry...and your hope in God."

Asha saw that he seemed worried about her declaration of faith. "Yes, sir, my parents set the example for me all my life. My father was part of the Green Beret team that rode alongside the horse-backed Afghans with the Northern Alliance. That's where he met my mother."

"Yes, I found that rather interesting."

"He also worked with Peshmerga forces in Iraq against ISIS."

"I'm aware of your father's contribution, Sergeant Hawkins."

"I'm sorry, sir."

"No need to be. Now, I want to focus on your attributes. This mission would never work with any male soldiers involved, understand?"

"Sir?

"As I mentioned, this operation could, well, take some unpredictable turns."

"Yes, sir, you're right. Sir, if I may…"

The president shrugged his shoulders and nodded.

"I'm sure you've read my record in full, and you must believe I'm fully capable of measuring up to this task, or you wouldn't have summoned me for this mission. You wouldn't have read anything in my record connecting me to religious activities because I don't believe in any religious institutions. I simply find inner strength from the Spirit of God. I'm a soldier, and I will serve my country and its elected president with all my heart, soul, and strength. I am not afraid of the enemy, sir."

"There's one thing I want to be clear about with you. I'm aware of your training incident during your qualification course, and I still believe that you're more than deserving of wearing the Green Beret you earned."

"Thank you, sir. I've put that behind me now."

"Yes, I am sure you have, and that is good to know."

I see it as an experience like Joseph's trials in Egypt."

"How's that?"

"What was intended for me as harm, God intended it for good to accomplish what is now happening, the saving of many lives."

"Interesting perspective, Sergeant Hawkins." The president allowed himself to smile. "I have every bit of confidence in you and believe you will indeed accomplish this mission…but not without my—our help."

"Yes, sir."

"Now that I have broached this subject, studied your responses and reactions, I believe that my—the First Lady's intuition was correct about you leading this operation."

"Thank you, sir. I believe in this mission with my heart and will not let you down."

The president looked at her with concern. "I want you to remember that you will be going into a Gray Zone. My staff will take you from here and set you up in a nearby living complex that I believe will be to your liking. In fact, it is within walking distance. You will live there throughout the planning and preparation period, and you must not discuss this with anyone, not even family members, during this time."

Asha seemed offended that the president would even think she would divulge any information of this nature. "No problem there, sir."

"Good, I just had to add that as a precaution. You may call your family to let them know that you will be out of the net for a period. You must understand that anyone close to you could be in jeopardy once you embark on this mission. They will understand. Special Forces run deep in your family, and any lack of contact will not bother them too much."

"What about my team, my unit, sir?"

"The chairman is overseeing that. Listen carefully. You will be in full top-secret mode, answerable only to the chairman and myself. Do I make myself clear, Sergeant Hawkins?"

"Yes, sir, you do."

"Good. I want you to settle in your new place. Do you like seafood, Asha?" The president used her first name without the associated rank for the first time.

"Yes, sir, I do."

"Tomorrow evening, you, the First Lady, and I will have a nice, quaint dinner together at the Sea Catch. We'll arrange for pick-up at 7:00 PM, or as you soldiers say, nineteen hundred."

Asha chuckled. "Yes, sir."

The president stood up, prompting Asha to spring from the couch next to him. She followed him as he walked towards the door, which opened for them from the other side. "We have much to discuss. I look forward to our dinner tomorrow evening. The First Lady will be excited to see you again."

"Thank you, Mr. President. I look forward to seeing the First Lady."

As the president was closing the door, he could hear the Secret Service member tell Asha, "Right this way, Sergeant Hawkins, we have everything already arranged."

A black limousine waited outside the north portico where Asha was led by four Secret Service members, one of them a female agent, different from the one that met her at the airport. They ushered her past the two double columns at the Entrance Hall and straight through the opened limo door.

After a couple of quick turns, the vehicle stopped on H Street, just off Pennsylvania Avenue, in front of AKA Whitehouse. The female agent along with another male agent escorted Asha through the main lobby, past the front desk and up the elevator to the eleventh floor. When the doors opened, Asha followed them to one of the penthouse suites.

"Well, Sergeant Hawkins, this is home for a while."

Asha looked at the agent. "Wow!"

The agent stretched out her arm and said, "Go ahead. All yours. You should find everything you need here. Your personal belongs are here already."

Asha stepped inside and looked around the eloquent living area, which was spacious enough for more than one person. Painted in a warm brown and steel color palette, the rooms contained the latest customized contemporary furnishings, adorned with hand-appointed fabrics. A tranquil wall covering embellished the geometric-inspired carpet.

As she walked towards the master bedroom, the luxurious king size bed and leather club chair enamored her. There was even a second bedroom, which featured a plush queen size bed. The fully equipped kitchen featured stainless steel appliances, limestone countertops and a full complement of fashionable kitchen accessories.

Her new bathroom provided ample space along with deluxe jacquard towels, fine linens, and Bulgari amenities. Additional conveniences included a Bosch washer and dryer, walk-in closet, and hardwood floors.

"I could get very used to these quarters," Asha said to the agent.

"This will be your living area for as long as the president has directed. There is a sealed folder on the coffee table for your eyes only. I was instructed to tell you to read its entire packet within 48 hours."

Asha walked to the table and looked at the packet. "Hmm, a little more than an inch thick; not too bad."

"I will be down the hall, and there are four others on the floor below us."

Looking surprised, Asha asked, "All of you will be staying here on my account?"

"Yes. The five of us have been assigned to you until directed otherwise."

"I'm very appreciative," she managed, looking a little puzzled.

"And by the way, if I may say so." The agent lowered her voice to a whisper.

"It is quite an honor to serve and protect *The Millennial Girl*."

Asha stared at her and grinned. "Am I allowed to know your name?"

"It's Amanda. Remember, I am just down the hall." She handed her a card. "Here's my number." The agent closed the front door behind her, leaving Asha standing in the foyer, a little bewildered.

Asha turned to the refrigerator and grabbed bottled water. Next, she sat down on the sofa, removed her shoes, and reached for the sealed packet. Holding it in her hands, she studied the front and back before busting the seal open.

SEVEN – Smith Cybernetics

The silver jet made its final approach into a remote landing strip. It was a private jet, a Piaggio P200 Avanti, owned by Stan Smith.

Smith was a former Cybernetics expert with the U.S. Government before he became one of the three richest men in the world. A pioneer in robots, he and the best scientist's money could buy, designed the most unique and intricate humanoids that could not be distinguished from a real human.

The cargo on the aircraft, however, was human…real humans. The flight crew consisted of four well-armed strongmen, three women in their thirties, and five American teenage girls.

The five teenagers huddled in a secluded part of the tail section behind locked doors. They were still asleep when the private jet dipped its nose in a gradual descent as the sweltering sun sunk over the desert terrain.

Sleepy-eyed Nicole peeled back the curtain next to her luxurious bed. Seeing the sun fade below a sea of sand in the distance, she gasped! "My God! Where are we?"

A blue-eyed, blonde-haired girl shot up and grabbed the curtain out of Nicole's hand. With a panic-stricken voice, she exclaimed, "We're in a desert."

A third girl, who seemed younger than Nicole, began to cry while a fourth jumped up and ran for the door, frantically turning the knob. A fifth girl still lay sleeping on the bed, not moving. The door swung open from the outside, and a tall woman with dark hair stood in the doorway. Behind her, a large, muscle-bound man stood bearing his arms along with a strapped pistol on his side.

"Good evening, girls," the woman began. "My name is Stella, and I will be your hostess and your guide throughout your stay with us." She wanted to continue as if on cue but stopped. "There, there, young lady, there is no need to cry. Everything will be fine, you'll see." The young girl sobbed louder, prompting Stella to take two swift steps towards her before slapping the girl across the face.

"Who are you? Where are we?" the older blonde girl yelled as she wrapped her arms around the youngest girl, who was stricken with horror.

"You! All of you will begin to show some manners this instant!" the woman snapped. The muscular man stepped into the room, crossing his arms. "Or else we shall have to teach all of you how to behave."

"I—I just want to know where we are and who you are."

"In time, my dear, in time. Now, as I was saying, I will train each one of you…" The woman stopped again and glared at the girl who was still sleeping. "Somebody wakes her up."

Nicole shook the girl's shoulder. She was the smallest and youngest of the five. "Come on, wake up, little one," Nicole said with rising concern. Looking at the lady who called herself Stella, Nicole raised her voice. "She's not moving! Oh, my God! What did you do to her?"

"That will be enough. Ivan, get Leslie, now! Hurry!"

The man spun around and vanished from the room, coming back seconds later behind a red-haired woman. She brushed past the girl standing by the door and leaned forward next to Stella, who was administering life-saving measures to the sleeping girl. Leslie had a syringe in her hand, and she administered an injection into the girl's arm.

"Is she dead?" Nicole dared to ask.

Neither woman answered, prompting Nicole to clutch the arm of the blonde girl, who looked back with a tear trickling down her face as she shrugged her shoulders.

Just then, another well-built man entered the room. "Well?"

Both women stood up together. Leslie answered, "She's going to make it."

"Good. The captain wants us to prepare for landing."

"Of course." Leslie left the room with the second man.

"Now, then. She will be all right, but you all must take a seat in those chairs and place your seatbelt on before we land. It's for your own safety."

"Like she's really concerned," the blonde-haired girl whispered to Nicole.

All four girls who were awake looked to where Stella was pointing and moved towards the leather chairs. "Hurry along, now."

Each girl took a seat, strapped their belts on and watched as Stella scooped the still unconscious girl from the bed and positioned her in a reclining chair. The girl's arms draped over Stella's shoulders as she strapped her in place.

"Are you sure she's, okay?" The blonde-haired person asked.

"That is none of your concern at the moment, young lady."

The man still standing in the room glared at the blonde-haired girl and allowed a hideous grin to crease his face, causing her to turn away.

Several weeks later, Nicole again peeled back the curtain…this time from a luxurious bed in a hotel room at a place that sat somewhere in a desert. Below her was a large casino. Her glassy eyes gazed down at a middle-aged customer as he gave Stella a handful of American dollars.

Nicole had once appealed to a customer who was obviously an American during her first week working as a table server. She had hoped he would try to rescue her. "I'm not here by choice," she whispered to the American, who was a professional executive.

"Oh? How did you get here? Are you not one of the interns hired by Smith Robotics, Inc.?"

"No, sir," she whispered. "I was kidnapped, along with four other girls."

The man started laughing. "Now, that's a good one!" He elbowed the man next to him and shouted, "Hey Joe, this girl said she was kidnapped!"

Nicole tried to slither away, leaving their boisterous laughter behind her, echoing like a manic joker. However, she did not get far before one of the bouncers grabbed her by the arm and led her to a back room where Stella was sitting.

"So, you are trying to cause trouble, I see."

"No. The guy was drunk, that's all!" she answered, terrified.

"If it were not for the fact that you are being preserved for a special project, I would turn you over to these low-lifers now. Instead, I will hold you in isolation for one week."

"But—but isolation? What does that mean?"

Nicole, like the others, sought unusual ways to escape and naively thought that well-dressed American men were trustworthy. To her repugnance, she discovered that they were there for one purpose…which led to her mistrust of everyone.

Makeala, the blonde girl who arrived with Nicole, sat in a corner of the dark isolation room. Nicole watched her. "Makeala. Makeala!"

She did not look up.

"Makeala, are you okay?"

"No," she mumbled without moving her head from between her propped legs.

"What—what happened to you?"

Makeala sniffled. "I—I don't know."

"What? How could you not know?"

"I was sleeping…but not asleep."

"What? That makes no sense."

"Just—just leave me alone."

Nicole surmised that something traumatic must have happened that transformed this spirited girl into a devastated creature.

"Makeala, are you sure there's nothing I can do for you?"

Makeala lifted her head and stared at Nicole with a distant blank look. "Food. Plea—ase," she stuttered.

"Yes, of course! They left a plate for you here." Nicole sat down beside her and forked a bite from her plate. Then she moved it towards Makeala's mouth. At first, she did not move her lips, which remained shut. Then she looked over at

Nicole, who gave her a reassuring smile. "Come on. You can do it."

She smiled, nodded her head, and opened her mouth, allowing Nicole to place some food in her. Makeala chewed, wincing between bites.

"Oh my God, Makeala, did they do something to your mouth?"

She shook her head up and down, raised her hand, placing it on Nicole's, and motioned for Nicole to continue.

Nicole nodded her approval. "Okay, I will keep feeding you. You'll tell me if something hurts and when to stop, right?"

Makeala smiled again and nodded her head.

"Okay, girl. Let's do this and get you back to being Makeala." Tears rolled down her cheek as she continued giving her friend some food.

Makeala reached over and placed her hand on Nicole's cheek to wipe them away. Then she smiled and shook her head sideways, whispering, "Be strong, girl."

EIGHT - Mission

Inside the folder, there was a large 8 x 10 black and white photo of a teenage girl. A caption at the bottom read:

Nicole Anderson, Age 14.
Missing on September 21, 2025.
Whereabouts: Unknown.

She studied the photo of Nicole and closed her eyes. "Lord, help me find this girl alive and safe." Then more to herself she uttered, "Let's find out what leads there are, shall we?"

There were four other photos, each identical to Nicole's with a photo, name, age, and date missing. Asha noted two things that struck her the most: the same general area and the same period that all five girls went missing suggested an obvious connection. The youngest girl,

Karen, was eleven years old. The oldest, Makeala, was sixteen.

Asha set the folder down on the table, stood up and walked to the window overlooking the streets of D.C. Lifting the blinds, she took a sip of water and stared out into the blue sky. "Lord, where are these girls? They have been gone for two weeks now. Time is of the essence. Help me find them and bring them home safely."

Picking up her forest-colored knapsack, she pulled out a lightweight, roll laptop that folded into a storage tube when not in use. After stretching the flexible screen out on the table, she reached back into her bag and retrieved a pen that she mounted with a mini tripod. Next, she flicked a tiny lever to project a computer display with a touch screen-like virtual keyboard on the table surface next to the laptop.

When she was satisfied with the mount, she went digging into her bag one final time to pull out a sight-impaired laptop with a tactile interface that converted screen images to 3D shapes. This one contained voice recognition in lieu of a conventional keyboard. The last part of her puzzle was connecting all the wires into the appropriate ports that would enable all three pieces of equipment to interface with one another.

"There! I'm all set!" she told herself while speaking into the third device. "Testing, one, two, three. Testing, one, two, three."

Asha reached for the control and played back the recording. "Perfect!"

"Time to begin *Operation Resilience*." She gave this name based on her approach to addressing the protection, support, and the sustainment of a mission.

"I want six main categories. Begin sequence." Although she spoke into the third device, the text displayed in English from the pen onto the table surface and in Russian on the first flexible screened device.

"Number one: Critical Infrastructure. Number two: Network systems. Number three: Military," Asha continued in a monotone voice. "Number four: Government involvement-good. Number five: Government involvement bad. Number six: Human supply routes. Number seven…hmm, number seven: contingencies."

It was a painstaking task but one that Asha was familiar with and…particularly good at doing. It was her own Work Breakdown Structure. Her dad taught her the basics of a WBS. She used it ever since, for herself mostly.

"Let's start with Government Good: A, Identification, and mitigation of operational risks. B, Preparation for backup support. C, Rapid response with functional command and control. And D,

Recovery, restoration, and exfiltration following successful mission completion."

Asha continued piecing up the puzzle, evaluating how she would implement the execution, appropriate decision-making, and most of all plans all contingency factors which would lead to adjustments.

"Schematics questions to ask: One: can world-class network systems be attacked? Two, can they be recovered? Three, what are the recovery-restoration points and are they achievable? That should be enough to get started. Break one."

By late afternoon, Asha felt restless and got the urge to go for a run. After changing into her running clothes, she began her ten-minute stretching and then took the elevator down, went outside and started running towards the White House. As she ran past the presidential residence, the Washington Monument loomed ahead of her, standing like a beacon.

Sensing another runner come up to her side, she turned to see. She began in that direction before she sensed someone behind her.

"Going somewhere?"

"Hi, Amanda. I knew you would be along eventually."

"Well, it would have been nice had you given me a little warning."

"Sorry. The idea was a bit impulsive."

"Could you at least stop by my door or ring me and let me know the next time you have an impulse?"

Asha smiled. "Yes, of course."

Amanda tried not to smile as she shook her head.

Asha decided to put in a little speed behind her legs, one because she loved running fast, and two because she was curious to see if the Secret Service personnel were up to par with the Special Forces.

Amanda stayed with her. Waiting for the right moment, Asha took off in a sprint. She slowed just enough to look over her shoulder as Amanda zoomed past her.

She wasn't stopping, so Asha turned on the afterburners to get past Amanda, and so it went…a cat-and-mouse game of running until they found themselves approaching the White House after circling the entire mall area, from the war memorials to the Capitol building and back.

Stopping at the White House, Asha said, between pants, "Good run."

Amanda coughed a couple of times and answered, "Yep."

Asha smiled and filed the information she wanted in her head. Then, they returned to their rooms.

On the desk where Asha was working, there was a letter next to her file. It was from the president.

Dear Sergeant Hawkins,

I cannot tell you how grateful I am for you to lead this mission. I want nothing more than to bring our American girls back home alive.

The human trafficking cartel involved with this atrocity must pay. Therefore, you have been given full authority to terminate with extreme prejudice those you find responsible.

I have given you my private encrypted number, allowing you to bypass any bureaucratic barrier. Memorize this code and then destroy this letter. It never existed.

The Official Presidential Seal was at the bottom.

Shadowed by her protectors the following morning, Asha went straight towards a Starbucks across the street. Before she entered, she turned towards Amanda. "Join me inside for a coffee?"

"Um, sure. Hold on." Amanda spoke towards her wrist. "3859, close."

"Roger, 59. Eyes on."

Looking at Asha with a smile, she added, "I'm in. My treat."

Asha smiled back. "I was the one inviting you."

"Listen, MG, I have you covered in every way!"

"Millennial Girl?" Asha asked, chuckling, as they entered the Starbucks.

"My code name for you—you know, *Millennial Girl*."

Asha shook her head, laughing. "Okay, BG."

"Let me guess, Bodyguard?"

They both laughed together like old friends. "You know, despite all of your accomplishments, I expected you to be…a little arrogant. But you are quite humble," Amanda added.

"Because I invited you for some coffee? I may have ulterior motives."

Amanda responded with laughter again. "Yes, because you invited me for coffee...and let me run with you."

Asha smiled and placed her order. "I'll have a Venti, smores latte, please, and anything my sister wants."

Amanda gave her a peculiar look and placed her order. She waited until they both received their drinks and walked to a corner table before she began talking again. "I mean, you are at the top, leading the way—the cause. So many women look up to you after your accomplishments. When I got wind of an assignment that involved you, I begged to be on it!"

"How did you know about this mission? It was supposed to be Top Secret."

"Well, it still is. I don't know any details or what you are up to, but hey, everybody, or at least all the women I know anyway, recognizes you when they see you."

"Well, I may have the heart of a servant—sometimes.

"I am just fascinated by your whole demeanor, your attitude, even after all you have done."

Asha looked at her as she sipped her latté.

Amanda continued. "I believe you are ready, but the president has given you 48 hours to bring back your initial assessment."

"You don't know the details?"

"No, we are not read on. We have certain instructions about your actions, movements, and most of all your protection. That's it."

Asha studied her further. "You were in the Marines before this job, weren't you? MV-22 Osprey pilot?"

Choking on her coffee, Amanda shot back, "How do you know this? Who told you?"

"I make it a point to know about all those around me—even my own sister."

"Yeah, about that…"

"I'll tell you in a minute—what I have in mind. Besides, I noticed the eagle, globe, and anchor tattooed on the top of your foot the other night."

Amanda smiled. "Yes, I was in the Marines for ten years. So, I suppose you know the reasons why I left?"

"Just what was in your file. I was hoping you would fill me in with the rest."

"And why would I do that?"

"Because you will not be able to be my sister, nor any part of my team, if you don't. Amanda, I cannot do this mission alone, and I'll need a good pilot."

Amanda studied her for a moment. "And you think I am this good pilot, the one who crashed her plane into a valley?"

"And survived, along with all the Marines and refugees you were transporting. So, yes! I want the best! I want you!"

Secretly, Amanda had hoped that Asha would ask her to be on the team. She knew more than what she led Asha to believe. It was not by accident that she was selected for this specific role.

"Okay! I'm in! It will be my honor."

Smiling, Asha reached out her hand and said, "Welcome to the team. I'm sure the president will approve."

"How many of us are there on this team?"

"At the moment, just you and me."

"Wait! What…?"

"There will be more. Oh, I forgot to mention, I am impressed with the way you managed the Osprey under those conditions."

"I crashed it."

"You were cleared of pilot error."

As if reading from a catalog or contractors manual, Amanda said, "With the speed and range of a turboprop, the maneuverability of a helicopter and the ability to carry 24 Marine combat troops twice as fast and five times farther than any of the helicopters, the Osprey is a great aircraft."

"Yes, it reduces the size of the battlefield. We now call it the VSTOL, which enhances our expeditionary assault support, raid operations, cargo lift and special warfare."

Amanda's eyes lit up. "So, we can play the mental cat-and-mouse game, along with the physical. I see how it is."

"I made it a point to know about the rescue aircraft I'll be involved with. Back in 1980, one failed, causing the failure of the Iranian rescue operation in 1980."

"Operation Eagle Claw," Amanda added.

"My grandfather was there. He was in the Delta Force."

"Wow, I bet he has a lot of stories to tell you."

"No. I never had the chance to meet him. He died in combat in ninety-three while in Mogadishu."

"I'm so sorry, Asha."

Asha smiled, pushed herself from the table, grabbed her empty cup and quipped, "Because of him and my father. This is why I do what I do...love justice and hate evil."

"Okay, I'm with you! 3859, open!" Amanda voiced into her watch.

NINE - Smith

Stan Smith, the American multi-billionaire, founded Smith Robotics, Inc., in 2017. In conjunction with his research, he owned and operated the latest futuristic prototype city on the outskirts of Dubai. Named "CyberSmith City," it was part of an experimental model of the future.

A six-foot, dark-haired man of forty-eight, Smith was firm and had a reputation as a womanizer. He also catered to the rich and powerful. Besides celebrities and corporate executives, high-ranking members of the Pentagon paid official visits to inquire about experimenting with cyber-soldiers.

A high-tech engineer and entrepreneur by trade, Stan's most recent success was the development of humanoid smart systems that proved to be the most intelligent to date. Since many government officials sought an audience with him, Cyber-Smith City was rarely without a host of dignitaries. His net value of $22 billion seemed to be an asset that enabled him to get by with many unethical practices.

Smith loved sports, and his favorite, which became the most popular based on the sell-out crowds at top dollar, was the Ultimate Cyber-fights held every Friday night.

These fights were held in a hybrid coliseum featuring Roman vintage architecture, gothic castles, and modern, futuristic, three-dimensional holograms and multi-laser-light displays. A retractable glass ceiling and floor completed the look.

Smith's very own champion fighter and image of the futuristic humanoid was a female android named Cyrix. Cybernetic engineers from around the world had pitched their own supermodels against Smith's Cyrix, but all returned to their homelands disappointed that their prototypes were destroyed, none coming close to measuring up to Cyrix's skills.

The creator of Cyrix, Dr. Harold Roberts, was greeting a sports reporter for the BBC at Smithsport. The standard background loudspeaker interrupted their exchange as it echoed, "Welcome to Cyber-Smith City! If this is your first time visiting, we hope you leave with a memorable experience. If you've been here before, welcome back! Your experience must have been memorable! Have a pleasant stay."

The reporter wondered where the voice originated as Dr. Roberts led him to the main rail station through a massive tunnel system. Dr. Roberts was tall and moderately handsome, slim, with thick, dark hair and deep brown eyes. "As I was about to say, my world champion fighter has never lost a cyber-fight."

"What makes her so unique?" the reporter asked while emerging from the tunnel. Surrounding them were trees, flowers, outdoor bistros, an Olympic-size swimming pool with a forty-meter-high diving platform, and even a golf course.

"You mean besides being very beautiful?" They both laughed. "To the naked human eye, it is 99.9% impossible to distinguish my created blonde-haired, blue-eyed beauty from a human being."

"Indeed. But what gives her the edge over the other droids in these fights?" he asked, still taking in his surroundings in awe.

"Humanoids!" Roberts corrected. "Well, for one, no other has ever been able to swim the 100 meters in 2.4 seconds, let alone run the 100 meters in 4 seconds flat!"

"That—that's amazing!"

"It's ingenious!"

"This—this whole place is incredible!"

"You should see it light up at night."

"With artificial laser lights?"

"Oh no, with the natural light from the stars enhanced by our special component of the Natural Light Tubular Skylight. It acts as a super reflective, mirror-like light pipe with a 98% reflectivity rate."

"How did you engineer it to blend with the glass covering?"

"The entire length of the pipe's interior is coated with the reflective surface that's responsible for bouncing sunlight several times as it travels through the tube."

"Very impressive. Back to Cyrix. How did you come about the concept for her?"

"I'm glad you asked. You see, my wife Sophie died. She shouldn't have. Such a waste."

"I'm sorry to hear that. Cyrix? She's modeled after your deceased wife?"

"In a way, yes. I made some touch ups, of course, some enhancements. I made her so that she would be indestructible, incapable of ever ending. I even added emotions—her sense of love."

"This is possible?"

"Yes, I made her with all of those attributes.

"That's amazing!"

"The latest version of humanoids comes with three billion components, plus a choice of seven million combinations of cerebral activity. Any humanoid equipped with such a brain structure could assume any one of twelve basic reaction-postures in half a second. It took me a period of just over two years to perfect Cyrix."

The sports reporter scribbled something on his flex-pad while shaking his head in amazement. "I have no words for this!"

The two walked through the Cosmos casino, trudging along the carpeted neon lit walkway headed for the tubular-shaped glass elevator. "I'll take you to your room on the tenth floor. You'll have an excellent view of everything."

"I very much appreciate this."

As they passed a couple sitting at a table for two, talking, smiling, and holding hands, Dr. Roberts smiled as he recognized all the subtle signs that lovers send to each other. Out of earshot of the couple, he turned to the reporter. "Could you tell which one of those two is the humanoid?"

"Why—no. You mean?"

"Yes. The female isn't human." Dr. Roberts skipped the part about the ongoing projects taking place in a classified area involving cybernetic replication experiments and human traffic victims.

Stella walked into Smith's plush office segmented by formal luxury, steampunk paraphernalia, and futuristic architecture; a juxtaposition design fit for a diverse audience. Samantha had ushered her to his desk. "I'm sorry to interrupt, but your latest experimental shipment has caused quite a stir in Washington."

"Oh?"

"One of the girls is the daughter of a bodyguard."

"So, we've dealt with plenty of bodyguards."

Stella glanced at Samantha before continuing. "This bodyguard protects the President of the United States."

Smith flew into a rage, jumping from his leather chair, sending it sideways to the ground.

"How could your handler not know this?"

"He followed H2's orders."

Smith swept his arm across his desk in one wide, sweeping motion clearing everything lying on it. "Is this fool trying to ruin our whole operation?"

Always seen at Smith's side, many wondered about the relationship between him and Samantha. The public relations director for Smith Robotics, Inc., Samantha Stone, was a well-groomed woman in her late thirties and was always prepared with a logical explanation for the young women employed at Smith Robotics, Inc.

In her soothing voice, she convinced the media that the young women, many of whom were homeless and starving refugees, were brought to Cyber-Smith City to be fed, cared for medically, educated, and employed.

"Maybe so. On the other hand, H2 could be setting you up."

"When he arrives for the AI Cyber Conference in two weeks, be sure to arrange a meeting with him...in my chambers."

"Won't his high-profile cause undue attention?"

"Not to worry; I have something in mind that just may work in our favor. What's the president doing about this missing girl?"

"Do you remember the media story several months ago about the first female Special Forces soldier?"

Smith smiled. "How could I forget? I wanted her to work for me. She has a degree in cybernetics…wait! Don't tell me! He's sending her after me?"

Stella and Samantha exchanged glances. "Our sources know that the president summoned her to the White House and then went undercover."

Smith laughed hysterically. "I bet they did!"

"What I meant was…"

"I know what you meant. I couldn't help it." Smith paced the floor. Looking at Stella, he continued. "Take care of your handler for good."

Stella cleared her throat. "Our guy, Chad, went off the grid. We cannot find him."

"WHAT? He just disappeared?"

"We believe he was arrested—unofficial like."

"You mean by non-law enforcement officers?"

"Correct—Navy SEALs. Your kidnapping victim's father is also an ex-Navy SEAL."

"Bloody fantastic!" Smith roared.

"It may be for the best."

"What—you don't think the SEALs will make him talk? Ha. You don't know much about the SEALs, then."

Samantha walked over and stood behind him. Rubbing his shoulders, she said, "In the likelihood that he did talk, you can expect to meet the Millennial Girl."

"Who?"

"The female Green Beret."

Smith smiled. "Indeed."

TEN - Amanda

Between her exit from the Marines and her recruitment into the Secret Service, Amanda Hyatt had gone through a series of evaluations. Her last mission in Afghanistan was a disaster, and she wouldn't have survived had there not been immediate medical attention given from passengers on her downed aircraft.

New technological medical life-saving techniques saved Amanda, both at the crash site and at the trauma center…followed by the Top-Secret bionic enhancements…one reason Amanda was able to keep up with Asha during the run.

Amanda's existing skills matched those needed by the Secret Service. A trained aviator for the department, Amanda was placed on duty at the AKA

Whitehouse to link with Asha, in the hopes that a relationship could be formed between the two. Unbeknownst to Asha, Amanda was a specialized backup for the President's desire to combat Smith and the Cyber-Human Traffic situation.

In a large mansion at the Mount Weather emergency operations center, Amanda entered the living room from the shower. "What are all those…pills?"

"You'll need these to continue your maintenance schedule."

"Maybe later."

"Now!" the well-dressed woman wearing black-rimmed spectacles said.

"Well, could you at least stop calling it a maintenance schedule? Makes me feel like a machine."

"I've been studying all of your X-rays. Everything is in order. How do you feel?"

"Like a million bucks."

"Ha…11.7 million, to be exact. No residual pain?"

"None."

"Problems breathing? Soreness? Motion pains?"

Amanda looked at her with a smirk. "Nothing. I feel nothing."

The woman, Bethany Lawson, peered over her rims.

"Come on, Beth. I'm fine! I'm ready for this. Why do you think the president assigned me to her in the first place?"

"Well, it wasn't with our approval. We felt…"

"That I wasn't ready and that you still need more tests. Well, you know what you can do with these tests after tests…"

"Amanda. We do want what's best for you. Please!"

"She'll need me—my special skill set."

"Being a pilot?"

"You know what I mean. I wouldn't have survived without Dr. Robert's bionic implants."

Beth ignored her remark. "Okay, your report is good. You better get back now before she starts wondering what happened to you."

"She won't worry, not her type. Besides, she thinks I'm visiting my sick niece, remember?"

"Hmm, another asset we didn't give approval for release. The president must want this operation to launch immediately."

"Well, wouldn't you if this human trafficking got really personal?"

"It already is personal, which is why we've stepped up our testing for both of you."

"At what point do you think is the right time to let this Millennial Girl know just who she may be dealing with here?"

"What, being a Secret Service agent? She already knows this."

"No, my abilities and the inside suspect."

"Whatever happens, you must not let these facts slip. It may be our only chance. I'm sure you'll know when the time is right. Just remember, all of you are on the same team."

Amanda walked over to the window, looking out into the Blue Ridge Mountains. The FEMA National Radio System, connecting with the federal public and U.S military by the president, stood in her view.

Amanda reflected on her past, her mission, the one that almost ended her life. It was in Afghanistan just two years before.

Sounds echoed in my head as I could taste the dust and feel the heat. I'm going up! I remember saying.

Hold! Hold!

Gotta go now! Incoming hot!

Please! Just 1 MIKE!

Come on! Come on!

CLEAR!

I raised the lever and lifted off from a hot landing zone. "What the...?" The nacelles failed to rotate forward to the full 90 degrees for the flight.

On board the V-22 Osprey, I was carrying a group of Marines, members of a SEAL Team, and Afghan refugees. The process of conversion took twelve seconds, but the aircraft was hovering after forty-five seconds, an eternity when receiving incoming hostile fire. Believe me.

I looked at the instrument panel indicators showing that the rotation had still not been completed. My first attempt to correct the growing fiasco was to reverse the nacelles back into hovering mode. A gust of wind swept across the nose of the aircraft, so I made a base turn into a strong tailwind.

Hovering at nine hundred feet above the ground, the broad mountainside blanketed by trees in the Afghan terrain rushed upward as the aircraft dropped to seven hundred feet. Managing my fear, I did my best to overcome the low inertia with the aircraft's rotors. Come on!

My actions caused the proprotor gearbox to fail, and the Osprey could no longer keep feathered.

I yelled, "Mayday! Mayday! Going down!"

By taking this last-minute evasive action, I shut down both engines in preparation for an emergency landing. Thinking about the passengers in the back, I maneuvered the aircraft the best I could to absorb the bulk of the impact towards the front. The aircraft dropped hard. That was the last thing I remembered.

I was told later at a hearing board that because of my actions, I took the brunt of the force and suffered the most traumatic injuries of anyone aboard the V-22. It was fortunate that Navy SEALs were aboard and immediately at my side, administering traumatic life-support. After calling in airstrikes that decreased the incoming barrage, another V-22 landed long enough to transport my passengers and me to Bagram Airfield.

Teaming up with Asha gave Amanda great delight. The POTUS had given permission, and Asha was relieved. They both celebrated on the rooftop with burgers and drinks before retiring into what Asha referred to as the planning room. She handed Amanda the file that the president had on Asha. "Here you are. Now you can read up on me. I'm going to review the new packet given to me today."

"I can't wait!" Amanda said while poring over the pages of Asha's life.

After an hour had passed, Asha returned to the living room. Amanda looked up at her with a mixture of sorrow, anger, and pride. "So, we do have a lot in common."

Asha shook her head, "Yes. The reason I asked you to be with me on this mission. You see, there's almost nothing that can be done to either of us now that we haven't already been through."

"So, you knew? How?"

"There's no way you could have kept up with me on that run if you hadn't, you know…been enhanced."

"Good point. What happened to those creeps that betrayed you?"

"Different things. The ringleader and the guy with the bat are still doing time."

"Good. It should have been life."

"It would have been better if it had because I know of some mad people…well, never mind."

"I get it, believe me, I do."

"They almost got off altogether because he had high connections…but then, so did my dad, and he made sure that both of them served time."

"Your dad. He's the one who inspired you to go into Special Forces?"

"Yes, he and my mom both."

"You know, based on this report, your family is your strength. But they can also be your weakness."

"How do you mean?"

"If the bad people cannot get the best of you, they will go after your family."

"They can manage themselves, maybe better than I can manage me."

Amanda laughed. "I doubt that. How do you cope? What makes you so strong?"

Without hesitation, Asha answered, "My faith in God."

"Well, forgive me if I don't share your enthusiasm with faith. You must have read my views in my report."

"Yes, I did."

"And you still want me with you on this mission?"

"Of course. Why not?"

"You're not going to preach to me, are you?

"Nope."

"Good. Then we'll make a good team."

Asha smiled. "His light gives those who sit in darkness a guide to the path of peace."

"Huh? What's that supposed to mean?"

"Oh, nothing. Just a quote from the word."

"Your subtle way of preaching?"

"No, of course not."

"Great. So, what's the plan?"

"*Operation Resilience.* The details are very precise and if not followed—people will die, even you and me."

"You have my attention."

"I knew I could count on you. The first major hurdle is to overcome organizational hurdles."

"Ours or the enemies?"

Asha looked at her as if to say, *No more interruptions.* "Both. Now…"

"I'm sorry."

"Now, I must oversee compartmentalization of the risk-management activities, such as information security funding, staff, and policy, at least for this mission. Questions?"

"No, ma'am."

"Everyone I select for this mission, and there won't be many, will be trained to perform their assigned roles. We'll rehearse our plan and contingencies. I'll address any skill gaps or noted deficiencies."

"Pardon me for asking, but do we have a team…other than the two of us?"

"I'm working on it."

"Oh, okay."

"Communication is critical throughout the mission, meaning we'll need the latest, most sophisticated comms devices available."

"I can help you with that."

"Our risk management training will continue throughout the mission in a way where we must identify new risks and how to prevent, mitigate, monitor, or accept."

"Accept?"

"Not as bad as you think, more like an obstacle that cannot be avoided but can be controlled. Incident management. We'll learn about this end-to-end handling of contingencies, those inadvertent actions to any team member or victim, including technological failures. The key here is the role assignments and individual responsibilities. We'll need dry-run rehearsals."

"I have a question. You did say there'll be more than just the two of us, right?"

"You said you could help me with that. I still need a cyber-hacker, somebody who's efficient in both penetrating the targets system while being able to protect our own. Anybody come to mind?"

"Yes, in fact, there is. My niece, Jericha. She just graduated from ITT at Owings Mills, Maryland, earning a BA in Information Systems and Cybersecurity."

"I don't want to place your niece in any danger."

"Oh, she's already used to it. She works for the FBI."

"Well, can she access the Internet with the ability to attack sophisticated computers and affect multiple systems by designing, configuring, implementing, managing, and supporting a secure reliable computer system? She'll need to gain unauthorized access to financial accounts and confidential information from targeted systems."

"Yep. That's her. She can do all of those. I can arrange a meeting with her today."

"And you're okay with this?"

"Yes, I am."

ELEVEN - Jericha

Asha and Jericha sat around the 14K Restaurant & Lounge, an outdoor café in the DC metro area on 14th Street. "Thank you for meeting with me, Jericha."

"Oh, the pleasure is mine, believe me. Amanda told me that you were the Millennial Girl! Wow, it really is you! I thought she was just pulling my leg."

Asha chuckled. "So, please tell me a little about yourself, your studies, your expertise, your role with the FBI in cybersecurity systems."

Standing at five feet, six inches, Jericha was smaller than Asha had pictured. She also could not help but notice Jericha's multicolored hair that began with bright purplish strands that faded to a bluish tinge at the bottom, resting on her shoulders.

"Well, I studied the Information Systems and Cybersecurity program. It was at the ITT Technical Institute."

"I've heard of it."

Asha took a sip of her Merlot as she listened. Although a bit distracted by Jericha's nose ring and tattooed arms, it did not show in her expression. To a passerby, the two would appear to be the odd couple since Asha wore a cyanine sea-colored knitted wool blend and a two-piece midi-dress to match her black pair of ankle-strap dress sandals.

Jericha, on the other hand, wore a black-flared, soft sweatshirt with a loose hood draped down her back. Underneath, she sported a combined black skirt and black leggings ensemble. A pair of dark purple, well-worn, leather combat boots adorned her feet.

"I was top of the class with a 4.0 GPA! A couple of my professors told me I was a natural."

"Wow, congratulations! I am impressed."

"Thank you!"

"So, critical asset protection—what can you tell me about your experience with this?"

"Well, I had to identify, protect, and maintain a high-value asset involving a confidential missing person case."

"And this involved a comprehensive threat monitoring and mitigation?"

"Absolutely. I would be, you know, *geehkk* if I didn't," Jericha answered as she moved her finger across her neck, tilted her head, widened her eyes, and stuck out her pierced tongue in conjunction with the noise.

Asha laughed. "I bet."

"I don't know if Amanda told you, but white-hat hacking is my specialty. I learned to become an expert at eavesdropping on open wireless networks because it is so easy to overhear something on the wires and people don't realize this." Jericha took a sip of her Pinot Grigio; the sunlight glittered from her arms and caught Asha's eyes, causing her to blink. "Oh, sorry."

"No worries."

"My jewelry is a reflection of my personality."

Asha smiled. "I see. Where did you get your necklace and bracelet? They are quite exquisite."

"Oh, thank you. The necklace is called, ready for this? A Vintage Princess Lace Gothic Necklace."

"Hmm, I love that Victorian black lace, how it forms into a drop-bead style."

Jericha chuckled. "This choker pendant is a Vampire Chain. It matches my earrings, see?" She pulled back her hair to reveal a pair of Wrap Dragon Ear Cuff, Stud Earrings.

"Cool! The design from Game of Thrones?

"Yes, in fact…wait, how do you know all this?"

"I have younger brothers."

"This bracelet is a Victorian Skeleton Key Heart Cross."

"Where do you get all of these items?"

"Different places but—never mind."

"What?"

Jericha laughed. "The name of the place where I get a lot of my wardrobe."

Asha laughed with her. "Okay, back to your experience. What about writing tools like password crackers, vulnerability scanners, and anonymities?"

"I am proficient with all of them. In fact, I can uncover flaws in any software

154 | SCOTT MEEHAN

by allowing destructive worms and viruses to gain access."

Asha studied her for a few seconds, wondering about Jericha's true motive.

"Something seems to be troubling you though."

"My past has not been easy. I don't know what Amanda told you, but I came to be with her family in the past few years."

"No, she had not mentioned it."

"Well, I lost somebody very dear to me when I was young."

"I'm sorry to hear that, Jericha. She was never found?"

Jericha investigated her glass of wine and mumbled, "No."

"I have a question for you. Please consider it carefully before answering me." Asha leaned forward and lowered her voice.

Jericha leaned forward. "Okay."

"Amanda and I engage in a Top-Secret operation, known only by the president himself."

Jericha's eyes widened.

"He has given me permission to assemble a small team consisting of those who I deem pertinent to complete this operation. I…"

"Yes!"

"You did not let me finish."

"It doesn't matter, I mean it does, but I want to be part of your team. Please!"

"The mission involves great risk with some very bad people…"

"I'll do it!"

"I did not even tell you what you would be doing or who we will be facing."

"Please! I want to go in, no matter what the risk! I can do it! I know I can. I am very quick at analyzing situations and responding with the correct actions. One of my specialties is hacking street cameras, to track down vehicles in real time."

"I am not surprised."

"I could have ears on you and Amanda with this." Jericha held out her bracelet, wrist side up to reveal a quarter-sized pendant. "I helped design it. I call it the Dick Tracy, or the DT."

Asha looked up at Jericha. "May I?"

"Yes, sure. Take a closer look. It uses a smart phone."

She studied the thin 30mm diameter piece embedded in her bracelet. "How many of these devices can a smart phone find simultaneously?"

"The average iOS model can manage up to 12 DT devices at once."

"Longevity?"

"Lifetime."

"How do I replace the battery?"

"Like this, watch." Jericha slid the back counterclockwise. "I call it the back door. It uses a CR1616 battery."

"Range?"

"Here's the cool part. One thousand feet! I'm still working on the antenna and firmware refinement, along with the cavity and power optimization."

Asha looked at her with delight. "Is it two-way?"

"Yes, it is designed with Two-Way Technology and can be used with other BLE tracking devices, Bluetooth cars, headsets and more!"

"How many of these are available, the cost, and are they all-weather terrain proof?"

Jericha chuckled. "That was three questions, and the answers are one hundred, fifty, and yes."

Asha laughed. "Excellent!" Then she looked straight into Jerichas gray eyes. "What I have in mind for you may be your biggest challenge ever. It will not be without risks. I like your state of mind, however, one that fits the role for just the type of hacker I need."

"I approach hacking as an offense, that is, from the perspective of the attacker. My methods are unique in that I gather a mental image, the big picture, when I look at how I can help secure an organization. I assume the mindset of an attacker, and rather than thinking how I can penetrate the business, I am wondering what I can do with my target once I've gained access."

"Okay, Jericha, you're in."

Jericha lifted her head, and Asha could see the large smile on her face. "You won't regret this, I promise!"

"I just don't want anything bad happening to you."

Jericha smiled and began quoting, "*Hippolyta built a nation of women, apart from greed and hatred.* You should have been named Hippolyta," Jericha added in laughter.

Asha smiled. "You read the Legend of Wonder Woman."

"*These mortals carved the path forward for their people...with words of peace, as well as spear and axe...*and I might add—computer."

Laughter erupted from both girls. "Okay, I like you, Jericha. Tell me. Are you afraid of anything?"

"Like what?"

"Anything. Afraid of anything."

Jericha thought for a few seconds before answering. "Yes, I am afraid of vast emptiness, like in jumping from a plane."

Asha just looked at her.

"Can I ask you a question?" Jericha continued.

"Please."

"Are you like Hippolyta in terms of weakness?"

Asha took one last sip of her Merlot, set the glass down, stared at it, and then looked at Jericha. "I hope not. I hope to God that I am not."

"Good! Because her downfall caused the demise of her and her sisters."

"Hmm. Yes, I am aware. I am also aware that we are fighting a disease—a war against our kind."

"I so want to be a part of your team, Asha."

Asha smiled and nodded her head. "We may have to infiltrate into our target area by…jumping from an extremely high plane."

"Oh my God!"

"Do you still want…"

"YES! I don't care about the plane."

"Okay, then. Um, out of curiosity, what is your hacker's name?"

Jericha smiled. "You already know."

"I do? Wait, Hippolyta?"

They both laughed.

I, Jericha Sloan, was born to a single woman who was on the run from her past. In the sight of the Empire State Building, my neighborhood consisted of garbage filled streets, dark back alleys, and cold winters. I remember them all too well, unfortunately. In my world of void darkness, either chaos, death, or survival was nightly routine.

My dreams were more like nightmares. They lasted night after night until I turned thirteen. I was taken in by the Hyatt family that year. It wasn't easy at first, but I adjusted well. Amanda was a big part of this transition.

After witnessing my mother's brutal death at the hands of three men in an abandoned building, I roamed the streets for three years.

My living nightmare strangled my senses, that—that vision of my mother desperately trying to fight off her attackers in a futile effort while I was too scared and remained hidden from sight— in a secret hideout. After the men left, I ran to her, sobbing, trying to wake her up.

"Momma! Talk to me, Momma!" I screamed. "Your eyes are open, but you are not looking at me! Your mouth is open, but you are not talking to me!

Momma! Please!" It was at that moment that I was no longer a child. I was an empty…nothing.

Time left my body, and I don't know how long I cradled the lifeless body of my mother. I just remembered how it kept growing colder and colder. I wanted to call the police, I really did…but in the past, anytime the police appeared, my mother went in the opposite direction. She was afraid of them.

Surviving in the streets came naturally to me; it was what I knew, all my life. For three years after my mother was murdered, I survived the dark back streets of New York, rummaging through garbage, begging behind restaurants, and moving from shelter to shelter. Since I was so young, I knew how to manipulate many of the social workers, acting as if I belonged to any random, strange woman, even calling them "Mom" at the appropriate time. Most of them didn't care and often played along...except for one night.

A counseling official from one of the shelters came near to check on me. Looking at the woman in the next bed, the man said, "You know your daughter could use a clean bath, new clothes and a medical checkup, ma'am. It is free, you know?"

The women looked at the counselor and said, "She ain't my girl. I never seen her before."

When she said that, I took off running. Although the counselor could not catch me at that time, he reported the incident and believed that I was a runaway. The counselor became so concerned that he assembled small search parties to keep on the lookout for me. I was finally caught and cornered. I felt like a caged wild animal.

It took a full year for me to assimilate back into a societal norm with the help of

165 | SCOTT MEEHAN

state-sponsored facilities and foster care. Like I said before, I was thirteen when the Hyatt family took me into their home and raised me as if I was one of their own.

I spent every day asking Amanda many questions, playing games, and otherwise researching anything that fascinated me with biometric security used to unlock a PC with facial features rather than entering a password. Amanda was a like a sister to me...a sister that I never had.

TWELVE – Young Victims

The historical and statistical portions of the documents given to the team contained background information on human trafficking. The girls read the report:

An estimated five million minors are enslaved in the global commercial sex trade, more than fifty percent of those belonging to Smith Robotics, Inc. The demand for younger victims grew over the years because of the uncontrollable refugee crisis, American, and European, businessmen engaged in "sex-tourism," Middle Eastern religious zealots who believe it is the will of Allah, Africans and Asians who believe that intercourse with a virgin will cure them of

AIDS and rich pedophiles from around the world.

Lucrative profits from the sex trade made it attractive to organized crime. Stan Smith saw it as an opportunity to not just make money but as further research into developing and creating the perfect humanoid.

Crime syndicates lobbied governments to legalize prostitution for increased tax revenue but also campaigned for no restrictions on the World Wide Web. For the helpless victims, many world governments agreed to their twisted logic.

ᛃ

Nicole Anderson found a new friend in Myra Singh. Myra's father had sold her to a temple priest when she was ten.

168 | SCOTT MEEHAN

Whenever the two were together, they swapped stories about their culture.

"I was not sold," Myra told Nicole one morning. "My penalty for being very pretty was having an arranged marriage."

"At age ten? That's—that's just unbelievable!"

"But the way it is."

"Your parents made you marry a man when you were ten?"

"No, not a man. I was married to a Hindu temple goddess. I became a *devadasi*."

"A what?"

"Devadasi, a temple prostitute. When the priests and other men slept with me, they believe they were sleeping with the spirit of a goddess."

"God! That's sick!"

"It was the way of honor."

"No way! You, and I for that matter, are victims of abuse! I don't know about you, but I plan to escape the first opportunity I get."

"When I turned sixteen, I was told that a new goddess, a much younger one, would take my place."

Nicole, looking aghast, just shook her head. "What did you do?"

"Since the gods watch over us and listen to our hearts and strengths, they whisper to us and tell us our destiny. There was just one thing for me to do. I was on my own, so I took to the streets of Bombay. I fit right in because young girls between the ages of ten and twenty lined the streets. When customers exploit the younger girls, they go behind the street vendors, beyond the dirty curtain, down stairways to tunnels leading to thousands of stalls..." Myra thought a moment before whispering, "...where the weak are devoured."

"That is so insane! I had no idea this kind of stuff went on in the world!"

Myra continued. "One day, an old lady took me to her church. She washed me, clothed me, fed me, and made me feel like a human being. I decided to walk towards the commercial section of town to sit at a coffee shop. Nobody knew who I was."

Nicole listened as Myra walked to the window, her smile fading.

"Have you ever talked to Monique?"

"No, I don't know who she is, why?" Nicole asked.

"She was at a refugee camp in Yemen, and a well-groomed young man came to her and said he was a secretary to a prince."

"He lied?"

"No, he was working for a prince, and he brought her to Paris, telling her she could make a lot of money as a model."

"But now she is here?"

"Yes, the prince brought her here and just left her. Now, well, as you know, she is not modeling."

Nicole looked down to the ground without saying anything.

"Same thing happened to me. A young man, dressed nice, asked if he could sit down with me. He was very polite, not like the other men I was with for six years. I did not know such men existed.

"Uh oh, this sounds too familiar."

"What?"

"The same thing happened to me in America."

"Yes? There, too?"

172 | SCOTT MEEHAN

Nicole nodded her head.

Myra continued. "We had cold drinks together, and the next thing I remember, I was on a jet plane! This is how I came to be here, like you."

"The lady who was on the plane told me not to be afraid, that I was going to be part of a great, revolutionary project," Nicole added.

"I was told something the same. These people have kept men from coming to us, unlike others. Did they ask you if you were a virgin?"

"Yes, they did, and I told them the truth! I am a virgin."

"This is why they will not let men touch us now."

"But you are not one; you just told me your story."

Myra placed her finger over her lips, her eyes wide with fright. She whispered,

"They think I am one because they do not know my past. Please don't tell them, I beg you."

Nicole nodded her head and assured her. "I promise. What do you think they want to do with us, then?"

"Maybe like you said, be part of a special project."

"But we are prisoners here, and I want to escape!"

"There's no way to escape. We are surrounded by desert. I am much happier now. Coming here to the Grand Plaza is like a dream to me. I always dreamt of such a place where it was neat and clean and where I could have a room of my own. I do not have any fear here."

"Well, this is no dream, it's a fricking nightmare! These—these creeps kidnapped me from my home in America! Taken from my family! I loved them!"

Nicole began to weep. "You wouldn't understand."

Myra placed her hand on her shoulder. "I want to understand."

Nicole cried. "There is something wrong with this place! It is full of evil and darkness from the inside."

Myra tried to console her the best she could. "I know what you can do. Tell them you want to learn Arabic."

Through her sobs, Nicole answered, "Why—why would I want to do that?"

"Because it will buy you time. They will put you through a course that takes sixty days. By then you will find a way out."

Nicole perked up a bit, accepting the damp towel Myra had offered her. "Are you sure?"

"Yes. This is what they told me. I'm surprised they did not tell you."

"I suppose it won't hurt to ask."

Myra smiled. "See. You feel better already because you have a glimmer of hope. This is how we must survive."

Nicole forced a smile. "Okay. I'll try." Then without warning, she began crying again. "Oh God, I just want to go home!"

THIRTEEN – Final Instructions

Three days after the president handed Asha a thick folder containing all the materials involving the mission, available assets, networking, and a host of other information, she was ready to present her plan of action. Asha concluded that the human traffic industry could in fact be destroyed, but not without conditions being fulfilled. She made sure that all the details were in place before she reported to the president at his request.

The president's staff filled the Oval Office when the intercom buzzed. "Mr. President, Sergeant Hawkins is here."

"Alright, thank you." Turning to those in the room. "We'll adjourn for now, until further notice."

Although everyone there looked at each other in surprise, none dared to ask questions, and nobody wasted any time jumping to their feet. As each moved towards the door, the president said his formal farewells as he walked them out until the last one departed. Pushing the remote, the president said, "Send her in."

Asha was dressed eloquently in a charcoal-colored bodycon-dress as the president greeted her warmly and motioned her towards the couch. Then, grabbing two bottles of water from the refrigerator, he handed her one and sat across from her in his chair.

"So, I trust everything has been to your satisfactory at the AKA?"

"Yes, sir, very much so, thank you."

"Well, I can hardly wait to hear your full assessment on this matter. Just give it to me straight and honest."

"Yes, sir." *Here goes,* Asha thought, recalling a rehearsed speech. "Mr. President, I agree with you that I will need total independence for any action within the sphere of unconditional secrecy. I will require presidential authority giving me powers supreme."

"I'm listening."

"These powers must enable me to receive, without objections, complete cooperation from any other agency or military unit whose cooperation is vital."

Asha paused to sip water for a dry mouth caused by adrenaline rushing through her mental emotions.

"Continue."

"I have recruited two others on the team, as you have been made aware, and we will need a budget of at least one hundred million dollars to be disbursed without any red tape, access to weapons of my choice, and ninety days to complete the mission."

The president coughed. "One hundred million dollars?" the president repeated.

Asha squirmed a little. "Yes, Mr. President, one hundred million dollars disbursed without any, you know, traceable bureaucracy."

The president took a swig of water and cleared his throat. Then he just looked at her, waiting for more explanation.

"Sir, if I am going to take action against a multi-billion-dollar empire, nobody can be forewarned with monetary transactions between banks or agencies."

"If I give you access to this kind of money, how will you make your purchases?"

"My personal phone. Mine is equipped with near-field communication, short-range radio frequency that will enable untraceable credit card transactions. I believe all stores now have NFC terminals."

"You make a compelling case, Sergeant Hawkins. Is there anything else you aren't telling me?"

"Well, sir." Asha moved forward as if to add emphasis. "There is one last request."

"Let's hear it."

"Human trafficking will have to be re-categorized from criminal law to a national threat, with the importance

intended to punish traffickers as an act of terrorism."

"That would take an act of Congress to change the law."

"Or an executive order, sir."

"Based on what?"

"An emergency declaration to address a public health threat, such as that which was done in 2016 for the Zika virus."

"I am intrigued, Sergeant Hawkins. Tell me how you would associate human trafficking with a virus?"

"Well, sir, an executive order has been issued in the past on human papillomavirus (HPV), a sexually transmitted disease."

"By whom?"

"The governor of Louisiana, Bobby Jindal, in 2008, sir."

"Okay, go on."

"He issued EXECUTIVE ORDER BJ 08-21 for a statewide Abstinence Education program based on a national study showing that forty percent of sexually active girls between the ages of fourteen and nineteen had contracted HPV. At the time, STD and teenage pregnancy rates were among the highest in the nation."

"The weapons."

"Sir?"

"What weapons were you considering for this mission?"

Asha looked nervous once again, not knowing how far to push the envelope. She already surmised during her prayer time that she would lay it all out and the worst thing that could happen was that the president would say, "No."

"Sir, first I would like to thank you for letting me choose my team and approving of my choices."

"You have a purpose, I assume."

"Yes, sir, I needed Amanda's close-range aviator skills, along with her Secret Service training experience. And Jer…"

"Understood. What else?"

Asha did not expect the answer to come back so soon. She cleared her throat. "I will also need a LW-EMP-4 with the computerized tracking system." *There, I said it*, Asha thought.

The president looked at Asha. "You do not want much, do you, Sergeant?"

Asha's eyes widened as she sheepishly shook her shoulders.

"The EMP-4 is a prototype. I assume you know how to use one?"

"Yes, sir, of course. I am proficient with it."

"Why am I not surprised?"

The president stood up, which prompted Asha to do the same. "Please, sit down. I don't want you leaving quite yet until you hear what I have to say."

She sat down, looking more nervous than she ever had, and took a quick gulp of water.

"I have always wanted to take on the big boys involved with this human trafficking epidemic. I have two daughters of my own. I allowed world events and politics to occupy most of my time, and it was not until I saw my personal bodyguard, and good friend, Bob Anderson, come apart when his daughter went missing. I would have acted the same way. Sergeant Asha Hawkins?"

"Yes, sir," she answered apprehensively.

"I have studied you through your record and during our brief meetings. My wife, uh, the First Lady, thinks very highly of you."

Asha's face turned red, and she did well to hide a smile.

"So do I, for that matter. And, I might add, your whole chain does, from the chairman down to your immediate commander."

"Sir, I—I'm flattered. Thank you so much!"

"You have given me a lot to ponder, but I am inclined to grant your request. For now, go back and get some rest. Tour the city and enjoy a fancy restaurant. If I allow you to go forward with this mission, based on your plan here, you will not have an easy road to travel."

"Yes, sir, I understand the risks."

"Even more so than I do. And you believe that you can pull this thing off, I mean destroy one of the largest existing cartels and save these girls from sexual oppression?"

"Yes, I do, Mr. President."

"And why is that? I mean, your level of confidence is far beyond any I have seen in most fighting men, and I have been around many generals. So, why are you so sure you can save these girls?"

"Well, sir, it is because I have come to realize that humanly speaking, it is impossible to be saved, but not with God. Everything is possible with God."

The president looked down at her and started towards the door. Asha, on cue, stood up and walked towards it.

"I'll look over your final plan, and we'll discuss this again in forty-eight hours."

"Yes, sir."

"I'll be in touch."

"Thank you, Mr. President."

He nodded. "Goodnight, Sergeant Hawkins."

The next morning, Amanda woke Asha from an uneasy sleep with a bang on the door. "Who is it?"

"It's Amanda, turn on the news!"

Asha jumped out of bed and ran to the door while fumbling with the remote.

"Check it out."

The reporter on the wide 3-D screen was talking non-stop about the president's latest announcement. "And so, with this latest development, the proponents for and results from human trafficking were re-categorized as a national health threat and would now be considered an act of terrorism, punishable under such laws as those that govern terrorist acts. Perpetrators will be treated as terrorists rather than criminals, and nations involved at the highest level would be considered enemies of the State and liable as committing an act of war."

The reporter rambled on as Asha stared at the screen, allowing a smile to crease her face. "You were behind this, weren't you?" Amanda beamed.

"I believe the president means business on this, and I feel much better about our chances."

"Congratulations!" Amanda yelled as she jumped up to give Asha a hug.

"When's the last time you flew the OSPREY?"

"Are you serious? I—I'll get one of those babies again?" Amanda ran towards Asha with her arms spread wide and would have knocked her over had she not performed a quick "ninja sidestep." Both laughed at each other's jubilance. "This is awesome, Asha! I'll love you forever!"

"There will be a lot of risk involved with this mission; you know this."

"I know, and I don't give a—I don't care. This is great!"

Asha's attention turned back to the screen. "The President of the United States stuck his neck out for this, and he'll face a lot of heartache."

"He did it for you, Asha!"

"No, he did it for the women of the world."

FOURTEEN – Final Training

Once the president approved Asha's final plan, she, Amanda, and Jericha began packing for their designated training areas. The president's secretary had given an itinerary to Asha on her last visit.

Each would be going to a remote area in western Virginia for two weeks of training, including at least one HALO jump. That depended upon Jericha's reaction to the first one. Asha and Amanda were experienced.

A HALO jump was the acronym for High Altitude Low Opening. In other words, jumping from a plane at high altitude required the use of oxygen. When the two weeks of training were completed, Asha received special orders from the president.

Based on recent intelligence from the kidnapper himself, three of the five young victims were being held at a secret and remote location in Qatar, west of Dohar. The POTUS wanted Asha and her team to conduct a rescue mission to bring the three girls home before proceeding further.

Since the operation was a rescue and raid mission, Asha's request to add four members from her Special Forces Team was reluctantly approved, but only after Asha laid out a detailed plan before the President. She purposely left out one of the members, Chris Short, her childhood friend.

щ

High above the desert sky, Asha, Jericha and four members of her team from Fort Campbell prepared their exit from the aircraft. A rigged equipment bag preceded the soldiers who exited the rear ramp one by one into the pitch-black sky. Each one wore oxygen masks and their night-vision goggles. Jericha had a laptop strapped to her back.

Asha steadied her body position and ignored the wicked wind and cold. Everything around her was green. Then, at the proper altitude, she deployed her chute and watched for the others to do the same. Feeling the violent jerk hoisting her upwards was always a good feeling. Asha counted five other chutes around her. *Good*, she thought. *Everyone's good*.

As the ground approached, Asha pulled and maneuvered her toggles and flared the chute at just the right time to make an easy one-point landing. Once her feet met the ground, she quickly reeled in her canopy, wadded it up, secured it, and crept to the rally point.

Soon, all six of the team formed together, one of them with the equipment bag. Weapons were distributed.

"Jericha."

"I'm here."

"How are you doing?"

"It was a rush!"

They all moved silently to their target, a long mud building containing the three American girls and one dozen guards. Heat sensors picked up two of the guards with the girls.

Moving silently towards their target, they used hand signals and whispers through their wrist comms. On the way, the team crossed over several wadis. Even with a cool breeze, the heat was evident, and Asha felt the sweat trickle down her face.

The mud longhouse came into view, and they all took a knee on Asha's signal in one of the wadis. She turned to Jericha. "Get set up."

Jericha wasted no time opening her laptop and prepared for the launch of the lightweight drone designed as a bat. Then she threw the bat like a paper airplane towards the building before regaining control from her laptop.

"Batman is on his way."

"Let's roll," Asha said. Five of the team moved forward, with Jericha staying behind.

The drone hovered over the members as they approached the building, rotating back and forth, silently keeping an eye on the team. All of them, except for Jericha, who needed to view the computer screen, kept their NVGs on and had pulled up dark balaclavas over their mouths to filter the dust.

Jericha took Batman in swaying patterns around the team members looking ahead in all directions.

Sweat continued to run down Asha's face, her nose felt clogged with dust, and she worked at avoiding a sneeze. "Talk to me, Jer."

The thermal images picked up ten signatures throughout the building, with most of them stationary. Only two perimeter guards moved, and their pattern was a simple march around the building.

"Ash, there are two on the move, one of them at your eleven o'clock, and another at your two o'clock."

"Roger. Eyes on." Tapping one of her teammates on either side of her, she whispered, "Neutralize them." The process took inside of one minute.

"Any other movement?"

"Negative. The three girls and two guards are motionless in the interior of the building, just inside the courtyard. You can breach the wall on the southwest side, just as planned."

"There are three vehicles at the opposite end of the building. Two are pickup trucks with anti-aircraft mounts. The satellite photos were quite accurate. Nothing has changed."

Asha sent three members to place and set charges on the vehicles. "Set them for 5 mikes, then join me back here."

They nodded and moved out. When they came back, the five of them took positions on the outside wall of the room containing the girls. The demo expert set a small charge on the wall to breach from the outside.

As soon as the loud explosion shook the area, the wall breach exploded on cue and four of them burst inside and immediately took out the two armed guards who were still trying to get to their feet.

The three young girls screamed in a panic until Asha ran to each and spoke to them softly. "We're Americans and have come to take you home."

Asha handed one girl to each of the three members while she and another provided cover to take out any reactionary force.

"Three at your twelve o'clock, Ash!"

"Got em," she answered as she pulled off three rounds.

Jericha was already bringing Batman in and packing up her gear. The three carrying the girls caught up with her, and the four took off towards the pre-planned grid coordinates where Amanda was going to pick them up in an Osprey.

Asha and the other held their ground, firing shots at the oncoming men.

"Let's pull back now."

"Go," Asha answered. "I'll cover and catch up."

"Not without you. Come on."

Both took off towards the wadi under heavy machine gun fire. "Aaahhh!"

The team member running with her went down, hit in the leg.

Asha kept firing back at her assailants and stooped to assist her fallen teammate.

"I'm okay. We gotta go."

Asha tried to help him to his feet, but he went down again. Looking back at the rising flames from the burning vehicles, she knew that undue attention would be drawn to the area in massive force.

"Okay, this never happened," Asha said as she hauled her teammate over her shoulders and took off running down the wadi. The gun sounds faded.

"Asha, come in!"

Jericha and the team made it to the rendezvous, but Amanda was getting nervous. "Where the hell is she?"

"Asha, come in!"

"We can't wait much longer. There are bad guys coming from all directions!"

Jericha looked worried. "Asha!"

"Get in, Jericha!" Amanda yelled.

"No, we're not leaving her here."

"We have no choice. Our mission is to secure these girls. Now get in!"

Jericha hesitated before entering the aircraft. "Oh, God of Asha, bring her in one piece now…please."

Amanda waited as long as she could and then began to lift off.

"WAIT!" one of the teenagers yelled. "I see someone!"

Jericha and the men saw a stumbling figure approach them…one that was carrying something larger than the one trying to run. The four jumped out of the aircraft and ran towards the figure, knowing it had to be Asha.

"My God, Ash, are you alright?" Jericha asked.

Asha didn't answer. Her face was coated with sweat and dirt, her hair matted around her face, and her eyes were in a daze. The three men relieved Asha of the girl she was carrying, who was now unconscious.

Amanda had removed herself from the cockpit and caught up with Jericha.

Between the two of them, they helped Asha aboard the aircraft, where she crumbled to the ground and curled into a ball. The Team medic already had an IV ready to hook her up and provide the much-needed fluids she needed. The injured soldier had already been patched up and was hooked up to an IV as well. Jericha looked at the three young girls, smiled and gave a thumbs up.

Ш

Whenever presidents wanted some privacy, they sought refuge in the cool, secluded lodges and cabins at Camp David. Presidents have entertained dignitaries, family members, and a host of others for more than 50 years. When Asha, Amanda, and Jericha had completed their training, the president invited the three for a two-day respite prior to the launching of their mission.

The retreat, once known as Shangri-La before President Dwight Eisenhower changed the name to Camp David in honor of his grandson, nestled in Maryland's Catoctin Mountains. The location allowed necessary seclusion and a perfect spot for the president's final words of advice and send-off to his special team.

Surrounded by trees, the facility consisted of several small cabins, a dining hall, and a swimming pool. Since several recreational opportunities were available, Jericha took advantage of learning how to ride horseback.

The president's guests included the three girls, the First lady, his two daughters, Sergeant General Sheffield, and the head of the CIA. Several Secret Service members accompanied all of them. Until the classified talks resumed on the last night, Asha, Amanda, and Jericha enjoyed spending time with the First Lady and her two daughters, ages sixteen and fourteen.

Standing beside the Aspen pool, the First Lady and Asha engaged in small talk. "We appreciate the invitation to this special retreat! " Asha exclaimed.

"I'm glad you three could come here for a couple of days," the First Lady remarked. "Both Mary and Tiffany are having a super time with you girls. Jericha fits right in."

Asha chuckled. "We're all having lots of fun! Jericha's like a weird kid, and she loves your daughters."

"I can tell," the First Lady said, laughing. Looking at Asha, she continued. "All of us appreciate what you are about to do. Saving enslaved girls and bringing back those taken against their will is a noble cause."

Asha was not aware of how much the First Lady knew about their mission, so she chose her words cautiously. "Ma'am, it is an honor to serve our nation in this way. It is what I do, what I live for, that is, doing whatever I can to free the oppressed from tyranny."

"I cannot think of anything nobler than that," the First Lady said as she turned to watch her girls and Jericha ride together on horseback. She placed her hand on Asha's and added, "Do be careful, all of you. Come back. Our prayers will be with you."

Asha looked at her and replied, "Thank you, ma'am. Your prayers mean a lot."

The First Lady patted Asha's hand, smiled, and started to walk away. "Come on; let's get something to drink at the dining hall, shall we?"

Asha followed her along the path.

After the two-day retreat was completed, Asha traveled to the Naval Submarine Base at Kings Bay, Georgia, while Amanda and Jericha left for a secure hangar at Wright-Patterson Air Force Base in Ohio. These two locations would be their destination in the United States before launching overseas towards their targeted location at Cyber-Smith City, UAE. There would be at least one more unscheduled stop for the team before reaching their final destination, however.

FIFTEEN – The Real Thing

The young, pretty woman sipped on a rosé wine as she sat outside on the balcony of her plush room. Asha made sure she had reservations at Hôtel Massena, in the heart of Nice.

Just 645 feet from the beach, the sea breeze caught her flowing strands as they rode across her eloquent face. A swift stroke with her semi-manicured nails controlled the dark wave of hair when she pushed it back behind her sparkling silver earrings. Without missing a beat, she continued moving the glass of bright red liquid to her soft lips.

Although the hotel offered the latest state-of-the art three-dimensional television on a wide sixty-inch flat-screen along with free Wi-Fi access and air-conditioned rooms, Asha preferred the outdoors on a cool autumn day in France. A heavy load remained on her mind, and she needed time to reflect on the series of events that had transpired over the past month.

Another vivid image came to Asha as she recalled a time from the distant past when she and her family visited this same hotel right after her high school graduation. Nice, France, was one place she had always wanted to go, and as a reward for her appointment to the United States Military Academy, her parents made sure she had that long-awaited trip to Nice. She did not want any part of going there alone, however, and insisted on her parents joining her. This time, however, she wanted complete solitude.

After arriving at the Nice Côte d'Azur International Airport two hours before, she wasted no time walking to the rental agency to rent the sleek new Hyundai

Aebulle motorcycle. Along with the aesthetics, Asha loved the Aebulle features—the conforming design that was inspired by the human body's muscular structure, a design that enabled her muscles to relax and contract when turning corners. She found a stunning red and silver model to her liking, and after producing the amount of cash required for a 48-hour rental, the agent smiled and showed off all the latest features.

Asha filled out all the necessary paperwork and then followed the agent to the lot. Spotting the cycle, she quickened her pace towards it and took a position on the seat. The agent, now joined by two others watched her examine the controls. "Yes, this one will do great."

"You have ridden one like this before, madame?"

Asha did not answer the question. "When this bike accelerates, my body will contract and become rigid, yes?"

"Yes, it…"

"So, I can speed through the tight streets with its specialized aerodynamic physique?"

"Yes, but…"

"D'accord, merci. Au revoir," she yelled as she sped off into the streets.

The other two agents began to laugh at the one left standing scratching his head.

The drive to the hotel would have taken less than fifteen minutes under normal circumstances, but always aware of her surroundings, Asha took no chances. Selecting the right mode of transportation was a key factor for conducting evasive maneuvers should the need arise. Part of her strategy included a spontaneous scenic route highlighted by zigzagging through back streets.

Thirty minutes later, she pulled up to the main entrance, where two young Frenchmen raced to her service. With a smile, Asha held up the keys and spoke in French.

"Qui est plus rapide?" *Who is faster?*

The older looking one of the two was much quicker to grab the keys from her hand while the other, transfixed by her beauty, stared too long, and smiled with a wide-open mouth. Asha snatched the keys back, causing the first man to swipe at thin air. Then, handing the keys to the younger man, she continued in French, "Parfois la course n'appartient-elle pas à la plus rapide, oui?"

The second man accepted the keys from her and responded, "Je vais prendre le plus grand soin de votre cycle, madame!"

Asha answered, "Merci." Looking back at the first man, she smiled and added, "Ne vous inquiétez pas, mes sacs arrivera derrière moi, avec la permission de l'Agence de location. Seriez-vous assez aimable pour faire livrer à ma chambre, s'il vous plaît?"

Delighted that he would be the one to take Asha's bags to the room instead, his vanishing smile returned, along with his answer, "Ce sera un grand plaisir, madame!"

Upon entering her room, she called for room service and ordered a bottle of Jaboulet Parallele 45. While waiting, she sat at the edge of her bed and removed her midnight blue Beacon Eastport Espadrilles, which gave her the degree of comfort and flexibility she desired for traveling. Then she fell back onto the bed, closed her eyes, and waited less than four minutes before she heard another knock at her door.

"Who is there?" She asked while jumping up and striding towards the door.

"Your bags have arrived, madame."

She peered out the door hole a brief second and recognized the young man in the parking lot she had spoken to earlier.

"Oh, yes, merci. Wait one moment, please; I left my purse on the counter."

"Don't worry about anything, it was my pleasure. I will see you later?"

"Oh, okay. Are you sure? I don't mind at all."

"No, no, it is fine. Ciao!"

Asha placed her bags at the foot of her bed, and just as she unlocked the first one, there was another knock at the door.

"Your bottle of Cotes du Rhone Rosé, madame."

"Oh, thank you very much!"

This time she was ready with a tip.

"Merci," the man answered with a smile and slight bow.

Asha shut the door, looked at the bottle, which had the date, 2020, and poured herself a drink. Next, she slid open the glass doors to the balcony and sat down for a relaxing drink. Taking in the sight of the clear blue waters of the Cote d Azur, she inhaled, allowing the fresh Mediterranean air to fill her senses.

Asha's secret mission allowed her free rein on how to conduct her plan. Although not knowing what she was up against, Asha's approach was the same as she rehearsed and planned. *Confront your enemies and determine their strengths and weaknesses,* she rehearsed in her mind. *Then outsmart and outmaneuver them.*

After finishing her drink, she went back inside and stopped at the foot of her bed. Opening one of her bags, she retrieved a motion-based camera, one that was Wi-Fi adept with her smart phone.

Her Flir FX camera was the size of a small ice cube and was capable of facial recognition. Flipping over the camera, Asha set up the 1100p caching video, which included a ten-gigabyte micro-SD card and a microphone. The FX was also able to record in total darkness with its infrared and illuminator capabilities. Looking around the room, Asha placed the camera on a shelf.

Going back to her bags, she next pulled out an iP2 Smart Gun, one that relied on radio-frequency identification when it contacted a linked rechargeable wristwatch. *The DT,* she called it, smiling at the thought of Jericha's invention. Asha placed the interference resistant watch on her right wrist and the pistol inside the lining of her fleece jacket. Then after glancing both ways down the corridor, she stepped onto the burgundy carpet and walked to the elevator. After passing through the lobby, she moved along to the open streets of Nice.

Her immediate plan was to walk the five minutes to the Old Town section and Massena Tram Stop. She proceeded without any sign of being in a hurry. Along the way, she would encounter the "water mirror" attraction, which was dotted with fountains and launched in random patterns, soaking everyone in the process.

She smiled at the thought of remembering when her dad coaxed both her and her mom into the middle of the mirror before unleashing a torrent of water on them.

She continued, passing by the Promenade du Paillon Garden, remembering the bands that set up for the jazz festival at the Théâtre de Verdure. Walking past the bizarre upside-down arch shaped sculpture, she kept moving.

Asha decided to walk until late afternoon, even strolling by the waterfront promenade, before heading back to the hotel for a quick power nap. Jet lag began to set in, and there was still an operation to conduct. After the all-day tour of the city, she came to adore, Asha walked back to her hotel unnoticed. Before sliding the keycard across her door, she first observed the safety measure in place, convinced that there was no intrusion in her absence. Entering inside, she locked the door behind her.

Her first order of business was to throw off all her clothes, which she placed in a pile at the bathroom door. Then, filling the bathtub with a soothing mix of temperate water and oil, she lowered herself into the back edge of the seat-shaped tub. "Yes, this will do just fine, Asha," she said to herself. Then she propped her feet over the edge, closed her eyes and reflected on the memories with her family.

One young man came to mind, a man who had grown up with her during much of her middle and high school years, a man who had been like a brother and she never viewed in a romantic nature. Named after his father, Christopher Short, Asha called him Christian.

As the tub water cooled and bubbles dissipated, Asha stood up and moved towards the shower, adjusting the handle until she felt the coolness of the drops cascade upon her body. Letting the stream rain over her body like a waterfall, her thoughts mingled with past pleasure and present danger. Thinking about her next move, she wondered about her mission— how she could pull it off with minimal damage. For now, staying alive was her top priority, that and making sure her team stayed alive in the process.

After turning off the water, Asha walked to the linen closet, where she grabbed a white robe, placed it around her, walked over to the foot of the king-sized bed, turned with her back towards it and fell backward, where she plopped.

Lying motionless, she shut her eyes once again.

SIXTEEN - Europe

The alarm from her computer wearable watch woke her from her dreams, and she rose to prepare for her rendezvous with a back-up team member, one that she had arranged for herself.

Riding her motorcycle to the *Jan,* a contemporary restaurant, she desired a good dinner and conversation before business. A drive to the Jazz Comedie Club would require a quick spin down Rue Lascaris, which turned onto Rue de la Malonniere. She could arrive at her destination in a total of five minutes or less. There at the jazz club, she would resume her mission…with an old friend.

"Nice set of wheels. Silver?"

"Thank you. Yes, why not? The words of the godly are like sterling silver, they encourage many."

"Good to see you again, Ash."

Asha smiled. "And always good to see you, Christian," she answered, laughing.

"Okay, if I call you Asha, you'll call me Chris?"

"Hmm, I'll think about it."

"How are your folks? Are they still in India?"

"Yes, in fact, Mom told me that your mother mentioned a visit to see them soon."

"Oh? She didn't tell me."

"How's Robert?"

"Doing well. He's almost finished at Ohio State."

"Good for him."

"Yeah, and how about Seth, huh? I knew he would be a professional something, just did not know what, but the NHL?! Wow!"

Asha laughed. "Yes, everyone is quite proud of him for making it with the Predators."

"As they should be! How about Caleb and Mariam? Everyone good?"

"The last I saw them, yes. Everyone is doing well, thanks."

"So, the official word is that you have been reassigned to the President of the United States."

"And the unofficial?"

"Well, word on the street is that you are either on some top-secret mission, or…"

"Or?"

"Or you have gone rogue."

Asha looked a bit concerned. "What? Rogue? You think…"

Chris smiled. "Don't worry Ash— Asha, I would never believe a word of that nonsense. My guess is, you are on a top-secret mission, or you would not have had that message delivered to me unless, of course, you are in over your head and…"

"Stop! Come on, Chris." Asha tried to relax her expression. "You know me. I would never become a rebel against my own country."

"That's good to know, and yes, I do believe you, I always have. There are a couple of old hats who started that rumor anyway, you know, the traditional troublemakers."

"Well, you know what is said about the hearts of fools."

"What?"

"They are worthless. Anyway, were you able to get that information I wanted?"

The waiter set down a plate of crepes while both smiled and exchanged pleasantries with him. Once out of earshot, Chris said, "Yes, and I have the materials you requested as well."

"I bet that was easy."

"I had to do some bartering."

"The stuff is at our old secret spot?"

Chris smiled at the memory. "Yes, the very place you…"

"Chris!"

"Never mind. Anyway, almost looks the same, except for more foliage."

"The old shack is still standing?"

"Yep, barely."

Asha chuckled at the memory. "What about the Zebra map?"

"Good to go."

"Cool. Sounds easy. Let's just hope nobody else has made the discovery."

"Yeah, about that. I am a little concerned. The company you inquired about, Smith Robotics, Inc. It is the primary political, physical, and monetary force behind human slavery."

"Yes, I am aware of this."

"They are very well-connected. Any clear and damning evidence would tumble his empire. And your mission? You will find such evidence?"

"That is the plan, yes."

"People assets?"

"Maybe, why?"

"Be careful, Asha. You never know what insider trading may be involved."

Asha smiled. "You have my six though, right?"

Chris looked surprised. "Sure, I mean, to a point. I wish I knew what you had up your sleeve."

"Like you said, Smith is very well-connected."

"Oh, come on, Asha. You don't think…"

"No, of course not. I owed you one."

They both laughed. He watched her a moment and added, "You're not thinking of infiltrating his domain as a refugee, are you?"

"No, not me. Someone on my team."

"Asha, some of these do not make it all the way to Cyber-Smith City."

"Thus, the reason I need this information. I need to find out the routes that do make it there without causing any suspicion."

"As you'll see soon enough, there are a lot of places involved."

"It has to be quick too. There is a time factor."

"Well, let me save you some time. All of the old narcotic routes from the western hemisphere go into West

Africa—the new unified state of SSGB, which is comprised of the old countries of Senegal, the Gambia, and Guinea-Bissau."

"Thanks, I decided to skip all those routes anyway."

"Skip Sierra Leone, Liberia, and Ghana as well. Same thing."

"The boat route is too time consuming. What about the ones from Europe?"

"I didn't want to say too much because this is a risky route."

"Risky?"

"Many girls do not make it to Dubai because many of the cartel leaders keep a large percentage of them for their own profits in Europe."

Asha frowned.

"However, there is one place where the flow seems to be streamlining from Europe to both Kuwait City and the UAE at Cyber-Smith City."

"Oh? Where?"

"Berlin. The eastern section, once controlled by the Soviets. A number of refugees who make it through a screening process arrive at Berlin from Madrid and the Ukraine."

"The Ukraine?"

"Yes. But Berlin is your key."

"I've been to the Ukraine. I wonder why the traffic is so heavy from there?"

Chris Short gave her a worrisome grin before nodding his head. "Or anywhere, for that matter."

The crowd spilled out of the Jazz Comedie Club, and Chris followed Asha to her motorcycle. "By the way, I do believe you are working for the president, or you would never have been able to afford these wheels."

Asha laughed. "There was never any doubt, right?"

"Ash...be very careful," Chris said with pleading eyes. The words danced in his head, *I love you, Asha Hawkins...as long as I can remember, I have loved you.* Those words never left his mouth, however.

Asha placed her hand on his cheek and looked into his eyes. "Pray for me, will you?"

He placed his hand on hers, keeping it against his face. "Of course, I will, every moment I—I will pray for your safety."

Asha gave him a reassuring smile. "I will contact you," she yelled, speeding away on her red and silver Hyundai.

The beachfront leading from Hôtel Massena merged into walking paths along the green countryside. Asha waited until midnight for the walk to the pre-arranged drop-off point. Much to Asha's pleasure, there were even more trees surrounding their "secret hideout" they discovered during their vacation years ago.

Wearing a black hooded, long-sleeved sweatshirt and matching quick-drying jogging pants, Asha had hoped she would not come across anyone. If someone did see her, she had her running shoes on, banking on the fact that a jogger would not seem too much out of the ordinary.

Once she arrived at the site, she conducted surveillance to ensure nobody was in the vicinity. Then she went behind the shack and followed the strip map to where the buried chest of supplies lay.

After finding the chest, Asha opened it and did a quick inventory. There were three Shadowhawk X1000 flashlights, three Shadowhawk tactical lasers, six cases containing small packets of makeup and mascara, six Zippo lighters, three helmet-mounted Ground Panoramic Night Vision Goggles, three tactical headlamps, three Garmin Tactix wristwatches, and a leather file folder, all of which would fit into her small backpack. The night vision goggles were the latest four-eyed panoramic goggles enabling one to see 97 degrees. "You did well, Chris," she whispered to herself.

The crackling of twigs disrupted her focus as she fell flat to the ground, remaining motionless. She laid still for five minutes before resuming her task. Grabbing the items and throwing them into her backpack, Asha slid away from the area, using cover and concealment to her advantage. Feeling as if the trees were watching her, she gathered increasing speed towards the beach.

Just before reaching the edge, she felt a thud that knocked her sideways to the ground. Though the force came blindly, she reacted with a well-aimed kick to the masked face of someone charging her for another crushing blow. The force sent the man backward, causing him to lose his footing and fall hard to the ground.

Asha followed her momentum and jumped high in the air with the full intent of landing with her feet on his chest. Her eyes widened as the man did nothing to move away from impact. Unable to change direction in midair, Asha came down with full force on the person's chest. The crack of the rib cage echoed from a direct blow since the attacker was already lying motionless. Removing the hood, she was both horrified and relieved—relieved that she did not recognize the man yet horrified about his blank stare into emptiness. She checked his pulse and confirmed he was dead.

In a hurry, she looked around for signs of another unsuspecting hindrance. It was quiet. Dragging his body into a low-lying wooded area, she grabbed her items, ensuring that the bag was still secure, looked both ways at the wood line, and entered the sandy beach in a full sprint.

Running along the sand with a heavy sack burned the calf muscles in Ashas legs, but she kicked them forward as high and fast as they would work. Stopping just short of the hotel to catch her breath, she walked the remainder of the way, watching for any potential onlookers. Convinced nobody was watching, she entered the lobby, went straight towards the elevator and then to her room.

Once inside the room, Asha changed her clothes and then went back downstairs. Walking towards the beach, she dialed some numbers on her mobile, and then returned to her room.

Grabbing the rucksack, Asha proceeded to lay the contents on a blanket she pulled from the closet. As she conducted a brief inspection, her phone vibrated. She responded and resumed her task.

Beginning with the *Shadowhawks*, she assessed the eight hundred lumens of light for each of the three high-powered flashlights featuring three AAA batteries that would give it 1,000 hours of life, and the fact that it was still workable after dropping it in water. Asha also liked the fact that she could zoom and focus its LED beam to see a great distance.

The other Shadowhawk device, the military tactical laser, was illegal for civilian use. Pointing this laser would send a strong beam a mile away. Besides using it to blind a would-be attacker, the powerful beam will point any necessary search and rescue operations to an exact origin. Asha thought of another use for the laser but decided to wait to discuss the feasibility of her idea with Amanda.

The ZIPPO lighters, not lit by fuel, operated without any butane. With no flame, neither rain nor wind would diminish its use. Recharged with a USB, the electric current begins with pressing a button that forms a hot X, igniting anything in its crosshairs. Asha inspected the lighters and murmured, "Tactical, practical and flat out cool."

She continued examining the gear and gadgets, reaching over to check out the two central intensifier tubes of the night vision goggles followed by the tactical headlamps. Another powerful beam from one thousand lumens would fit well since there were five different settings and a focused beam to pinpoint targets at eight hundred meters. Impressed with the upgrades, Asha placed one on her head and checked its 90° pivoting spotlight. Besides being

water-resistant, the headlamp gave the user hands-free capabilities.

Next, Asha looked at the Garmin wristwatches. They featured a GPS and a

TracBack. The curved, scratch-resistant lens prevented reflection, which improved the reading display. Continuing to talk to herself, she said, "This will be useful when I'm in a big hurry."

In her own opinion, Asha saved the best two for last. First, she examined the field surgical kit, making sure that the instruments contained synthetic Sharklet coating, a repellant that prevents up to 95 percent of bacteria.

She took the cases containing the small packets of mascara and makeup and walked to the mirror. Choosing one at random, she applied the make-up around her cheeks before wiping away more of the colored substance with a tissue, until revealing a coin-sized tracking device. The device had been in production for years and used by the general population to locate lost bags, bikes, or pets. Within the past couple of years, the military signed a contract and enhanced development for its use in many other clandestine operations to track people.

When her phone buzzed again, she exited her room and went outside. Walking towards the beach, she stopped at the water's edge. A young man walked past her without stopping. "Same path. Twenty meters back in a draw to the right," she said in a lowered voice.

The man said nothing and continued walking.

After waiting five minutes, she went back to her room to complete her task. Continuing with her acquired "Christmas list," courtesy of the same friend who was on the beach, she packed everything away in her gym bag except for the lighters and six small makeup pouches. Then she opened the file folder and regarded the information while fighting to keep her eyes open, her head bobbing in the process.

Four hours later, noises in the corridor startled her awake. Glancing at her watch, she gasped, "Oh my God!" before jumping up and changing into her motorcycle outfit.

SEVENTEEN – Team Compromised

An attractive girl with shoulder-length, light brown hair sat in a cushioned chair, her bare feet propped over the rail outside a modest apartment. Wearing a black crossover drapery, stretch-knit top, and combined elastic-wait skirt with leggings, she held a glass of mango juice in her hand as she watched the sun lifting from the horizon.

The terrace overlooked Monaco, which was nestled within the French Riviera and Mediterranean Sea. Her intense brown eyes refocused on a figure winding up the road on a high-speed motorcycle.

She watched the sleek silver and red Hyundai Aebulle come to a stop below her as its female rider dismounted and removed her helmet. Tilting her head skywards, the girl looked straight at her. "Hello, Amanda."

"Hey, Asha! Long time, no see. You have the key to get in?"

"Of course. Stay where you are, I want to enjoy the same view."

"Come on up. The coffee is on."

"Thanks! You're a doll!"

Amanda smiled as she went back inside to fix two cups of coffee. Asha came strolling in as she was pouring the second cup. "Well, how was the date?"

"Productive. But…"

"But?"

"The pickup was compromised."

"WHAT? Who?"

"I don't know yet. Someone's checking into it for me. I have the items though and was able to leave without any further interference."

"So, we can continue as planned?"

"For now, yes. I'll know more by this evening."

"I heard from Jericha, and she is in place."

"Good. We have much to discuss."

"I can hardly wait to hear."

Asha pulled out the yellow envelope and flipped it on the white, rounded table. "For your reading pleasure."

Amanda sat down and poured over the latest information. "Hmm, Berlin, uh?"

"Our best chance. I will meet Jericha there."

"And me?"

"Nothing's changed with you."

"And everything is set?"

"Yes. Why do you ask?"

"Well, I don't know. There's something in this report that does not seem quite right."

"Oh? What would that be?"

"You did read about the Homeland Security Secretary being in Cyber-Smith City?"

"Yes, I did. I thought it a bit suspicious, but not enough to alter our plans."

"Here's the problem. This group from the Homeland Security Department includes all three directors, the one from the Office of Biometric Identity Management, one from the Office of Cyber and Infrastructure Analysis, and one from the Office for Science and Technology."

"Yes. This fact had not escaped my attention, the reason for highlighting that particular section."

"But here's the kicker. The Under Secretary for the Office of Intelligence and Analysis will be with them!"

"I saw that too. So what? Is this a problem?"

Amanda stood up. "Could be. He knows Jericha."

"What? How?"

"He tried to recruit her for a position within his own agency. David Cranston is his name. He was quite tenacious."

"Oh my gosh, Amanda! Wait—wait a minute. This could work in our favor!"

"What do you mean?"

"We would not need to attempt an infiltration through Berlin. She could travel with us, as a company representative. This Cranston guy could be her way inside the network instead of inserting her as a victim!"

"You're assuming that Cranston has an inside track."

"Based on this report, the Homeland team is scheduled to meet with Smith himself."

"I don't know, Asha. Seems a bit risky, I mean, what if he becomes suspicious of her presence? Our whole operation could be blown out of the water."

"He would not suspect Jericha being a part of any type of operation. The FBI does not get involved with overseas operations. He would think that she just wanted to take a vacation at Cyber-Smith City."

Amanda thought for a moment. "You have a point, until Cranston gets paranoid and thinks she is following him."

"You believe the original plan would work better? I never felt good about that one."

244 | SCOTT MEEHAN

"And this plan?"

"I like it better. Less risky for her."

"What about the mission?"

"Do you know why this David character was so persistent about Jericha working for him?"

Amanda smiled. "Well, if you were to listen to Jericha, he couldn't keep his eyes off her and even asked her out on a date."

"Wait, isn't he a little old for her...and married?"

"You're right, Asha. This could either be good for us or..."

"Bad. However, think of the girls. All of them depend on us, whether they know it or not. Hundreds, maybe thousands of them. Amanda, we can do this."

Amanda gazed at Asha. "Yes, you are right. If anybody can do this, it must be us. We have the resources, the highest backing, equipment, and the plan. It does sound more stable than trying to get her infiltrated as a victim."

"It's settled, then. I will contact Jericha and make new arrangements." Asha smiled. "Here, I brought you a present," she continued as she reached inside her leather jacket pocket. Asha then handed Amanda a small bag of Florian Chocolates from the Confiserie Florian.

Amanda managed to smile. "Yum, breakfast!"

"A healthy one. Here, these are for you. I'll keep Jerichas." Asha gave her a small case containing the makeup kits.

"Are you trying to tell us something?" Amanda laughed.

"Yes, if you want to track somebody special, use these." Asha opened the one she had assessed to reveal the quarter-sized tracking device."

"Ah, of course. These will be especially useful."

Asha walked over to the balcony's edge. "You have a beautiful view of the sea."

"Peaceful too, that is, until a high speed, shiny motorcycle broke the silence with a wildcat straddling the wheels."

They both laughed. Asha lifted her head into the wind, letting the sea breeze flow through her hair. "This is a day the Lord has made."

Amanda grinned. "I was thinking more in terms of Mother Nature."

"Right. Shall we go inside where it is dark? I want us to look over the hologram terrain with you for the UAE."

"Let's go."

Drawing the curtains and turning off the light in the small bedroom, Asha unrolled the 2 x 3-foot sheets and laid them on a small coffee table. When shining her flashlight on the map, a hologram image of the terrain emerged in front of them.

"Wow, look how it depicts the topographical details, as if you were there in person!"

"Our team used these in Bangladesh for the full 3D effect, and the locals were able to recognize the area much better than with the old-style maps."

"I bet so."

"Our SF medics had their own three-dimensional version on human anatomy. We had this cool holographic image of the heart that was amazing! The villagers were freaked out, treating us like god."

"This helps in determining the heights above sea level."

As the two sat drinking coffee, taking in the Mediterranean breeze, and poring over plans, Asha's cellular buzzed twice and stopped. "It's Jericha."

Amanda leaned forward. "Is she okay?"

"Wait. Her message is coming across now."

The two waited anxiously since neither was expecting Jericha to contact them until that evening unless it was an emergency.

Not comfortable being a leader. I'm a better follower.

"What did she say?"

Asha handed the phone to Amanda, "She's being followed."

"In Paris? Who—who knew she would be in Paris?"

"Here, let me have it," Asha said, holding out her hand.

Amanda fumbled with it as she gave back her phone. Asha began tapping the keys.

Follow the instructor with the next set of exercises. Stay fit.

Jericha's answer came back seconds later: *Okay, will need a drink.*

Asha replied, *"My treat.*

"I'm going to go and get her!" Amanda said, looking worried.

Asha looked at Amanda. "No. I'll go. You continue with your rendezvous and flight plan."

Amanda nodded her head. "Okay."

"You are with me, right?"

She looked Asha in the eyes. "Yes. Get Jericha."

Asha hopped on her motorcycle and spun off down the road, where she would catch highway A6 back through Nice, and then continuing to Paris, a 589-mile trek by road.

The guide estimated a nine-hour trip, but one of the reasons Asha chose her current mode of transportation was to make up for any lost time in a contingency. Her plan was to reach Paris in six and a half hours.

The road hugged the coast towards the southwest before turning north on A8. Since it was 9:30 in the morning, she wanted to arrive before nightfall to give her time to arrange the necessary logistics for the pre-arranged contingency meeting.

EIGHTEEN – Overnight Train

Overnight sleeper trains linking Paris and Berlin have existed since the Second World War. In the 1940s, they took Hitler's troops from the Third Reich capital to the Nazi-occupied city of light. In 2014, the service had stopped but resumed six years later with newer technology.

Asha boarded the modernized Paris-Berlin sleeper, once identified by a grimy red diesel engine. The revised trains average journey time between Paris Lyon Banlieue and Berlin changed from twelve hours to nine and a half. The sleeping-car attendant greeted her in French at the door to the sleeper and checked her reservation. Then he politely led her to the room.

"Merci."

"Vous êtes bienvenue, madame," he replied with a smile.

"Il y a une autre fille. A son arrivée?"

"Aucun madame. Vous êtes le premier."

She smiled back and nodded her head. "Je vous remercie encore."

She looked around the two-bed deluxe compartment equipped with a shower and toilet. Soap, towels, mineral water & shower gel lay next to a complimentary bottle of red wine standing at a seventy-degree angle in a basin. Asha heard some oncoming passengers and watched.

Looking more anxious, Asha checked her watch. There was still time, forty minutes or so, but Jericha was already in Paris and should have arrived before she did. "Dear Jesus, please let her be safe," she whispered. "Come on, Jericha, where are you?"

New Age Enterprises replaced Deutsche Bahn, the German rail network that had previously operated the sleeper. Asha learned through reading the files that New Age collaborated with Smith Robotics, Inc. She placed a long backpack on the bed, which had fresh clean sheets, a fluffy pillow, snug duvet, and its own individual reading light. Behind her, Asha decided to convert the bed into a sofa, which included a small-extended table.

Pulling out her notepad, she laid it on the table, along with her plastic card key, and plugged it into the 220V power socket below the bed near the door. Then she sat and booted up her device and went straight to the special tracking system. As it warmed up, Asha muttered, "Come on, where are you?"

There was a light knock on her door. Jumping up, she opened it and with mouth wide open started to say, "Jeri…"

"Pardon, madame, mais vous voulez quelque chose à manger?" *Excuse me, madam, but do you want something to eat?*

The same attendant was there with a small cart of food. Not taking time to eat from her long, arduous journey from Nice, she scanned the tray. "Je vous remercie. Je vais avoir cette," *Thank you. "I will have this,"* she answered while taking a croissant filled with meat and cheese.

Asha pulled out a €10.00 bill and was in the process of handing it to the attendant when her computer started beeping. "Gardez le changement" she said while shutting her door with a click. Then she ran to the screen. "There you are!" A green dot on the special map showed rapid movement inside the train station.

Glancing at her watch for the sixth time in as many minutes, she saw the

255 | SCOTT MEEHAN

fluorescent numbers, *2051*. "Hurry, Jericha, hurry!"

The train, scheduled to depart at 9:00 p.m., showed no signs of activity. The dot on the screen was moving fast, the distance indicated that it would be cutting it dangerously close. Now Asha faced the decision whether she needed to make a hasty exit from the train.

Hearing the attendant not far away, she went out to meet him. Je suis très désolée, monsieur. Je ne voulais pas être si rude. *I am sorry, sir. I would not be so rude.*

"It is fine," he answered in English, catching her off guard.

"Um, so, you speak English?"

"Of course. How can I help you?"

"This train. It departs right on time?"

"Yes, we will depart on time. You are still waiting for a friend, yes?"

"Yes, and she's on the way now!"

The attendant looked at her, wondering how she knew but decided that she was merely hoping.

"I will check back in ten minutes. If she is here, good. If not, we must leave."

"Okay. Thank you. Thank you so much!"

"C'est mon plaisir," *It is my pleasure*, he answered with a smile.

Asha walked back to her room but discovered she had locked herself out.

"Great, Jesus!" she uttered, plopping her head against the door.

"Looking for this?" a voice behind her asked. Jericha stumbled with a large rucksack from around the corner.

"Jericha! Thank God! How did you…"

"Know you were locked out? I saw your reflection as I was tripping up the steps. Here, let me! I still think I'm being…"

Asha held her finger up to her lips. "Come on, let's talk inside," she whispered.

Jericha nodded her approval. She looked puzzled at her new surroundings since the bed was full of gear and the other side was a table piled with computer equipment. "So where do I sleep?"

Asha chuckled. "Just put your things here for now," pointing to the bed, "and this table turns into a bed after we finish."

Jericha threw her large duffle bag onto the bed and walked to the window and sat down just as there was a knock at their door.

"We are ready to leave now, madame. I need to see your friend's ticket, please."

Jericha opened the door and handed her ticket to the conductor, who did a double take after seeing the young pretty woman in purple hair, sporting a nose ring. He scanned the ticket and handed it back to her and with a tip of his hat added, "Please have a pleasant trip, madame."

"Oui. Merci."

"Are we allowed to smoke in here?" Jericha asked.

"Ha. I doubt it. Here, drink some of this. Asha poured some of the complimentary wine into the wine glass on the bar, filling it up halfway.

"No, all the way to the top," Jericha said without smiling. Jericha reached for the glass and gulped it down with one swig.

"Hey, easy, girl. Come on, sit. What happened?"

As they both sat down, the train jerked forward and slowly moved forward until it reached full speed. "So, this guy, kinda creepy looking, was tailing me at the Eiffel Tower. I didn't think anything about it at first, when he tried to strike up a conversation. I acted polite enough but went about my way, acting disinterested."

Asha had poured a little more wine into the glass and handed it to her. "Okay, that was good."

Jericha drank more of the red liquid and continued. "So, I left the area, got on the metro, and traveled to the square, near Notre Dame. I started walking around the shops, going downside streets and into various shops. And then I saw him again…watching me."

"Any idea who he is?"

"No, I've never seen him before in my life."

"Okay, you did the right thing. You are with me now. It will be okay."

Jericha looked at Asha for assurance and acknowledged her presence of strength. "Thanks, Asha. I am glad you are the one who came."

"This guy, did you see him again after that second time?"

"No, I don't think so, but I couldn't be sure!"

"Alright. Let's focus on what's ahead. Do you remember a guy named David Cranston?"

"Who?"

"David Cranston. He heads up the Office of Intelligence and Analysis."

"Yes—yes, I remember him. He was kinda creepy too. Wait! Is he connected to this guy here?"

"I don't know. You said creepy, how so?"

"Well, for one thing he couldn't keep his eyes off me...he kept trying to get me to work for him."

"Yes, Amanda told me about him. What else do you remember?"

"Once, I was invited to a reception in D.C., and his office sponsored it, something for a government internship."

"Right. They do that a lot there."

"Yes, but this guy, Cranston, kept mingling with younger girls—girls that were too young to be there in the first place. I thought the suits had kids or something."

"You mean like young college girls or older high school girls?"

"They looked like high school and some middle school. I thought it was weird. Creeped me out, and I didn't want to stick around. However, since I was in the FBI, I started observing more and stayed. Afterward, I submitted an Executive Summary report up the chain."

Asha went to her folder and rifled through the pages until she found a small photo. "Look at this picture."

Jericha took it from her and stared at it. Eyes widening, she stood up. "Yes! Oh my God! Why didn't I see this before?! It is Nicole, isn't it? The one we are going to rescue!"

"Yes. It is her. She was at the reception?"

"I remember her now. She was one of those young-looking girls he was trying to hit on, which disgusted me."

"You are sure she was there?"

Jericha looked at it again. "Yes, I am very sure."

Asha expressed dismay and revelation at the same time. Then she pulled out a photo of Makeala. "Her too?"

"Oh my God, Asha! Yes—yes, she was there too!"

"Jericha, listen to me. No matter what you think of Cranston, you must get close to him. He will lead us to Nicole and

Makeala, I am almost sure of it. He will not suspect you of anything unordinary."

"I can do it. I will do it for Nicole, Makeala, and all of the other victims."

"Look, why don't you clean up a bit, we'll go to the dining car, come back, hash over some information, and then get some sleep. What do you say?"

Jericha nodded her head. "I'm in."

While Jericha was in the shower, Asha studied her ticket and confirmed that there would be a one-hour layover in Frankfurt. She went to her computer and typed a simple message:

Need an Espresso at the clock. Let's say 0200? Then she waited for a response that came less than five minutes later.

Make mine a Cappuccino.

Asha smiled and shut her computer down and waited for Jericha.

NINETEEN - Missing

"Here's the part where you come in." Asha pulled out a portion of the information she had received from Chris.

"Just like all terror organizations, Smith Robotics, Inc., operates like a legitimate business. Smith has numerous financial flows, and you will get access to the routes. Once you get inside, you should be able to cut off all of his money flow."

Jericha fought to keep her eyes open. "This is easy."

"But to defeat them, you must first determine what countries and institutions are safeguarding his fortune."

"That will be fun."

Asha continued. "Next, you will infiltrate and monitor all of the criminal use of informal money transfers to Smith's networks."

"Okay."

"You will hack into the money flow system and freeze all of his assets."

"Sounds too easy."

"Maybe so, but it is rather complicated because cutting off large sums of money to shut down an operation will gain a lot of attention from around the world."

"I bet it will."

"This is why I asked the president for such a large amount of money, along with those cool weapons."

Jericha laughed. "And Amanda's bird!"

"Although the network is too widespread to trace all of them, we will focus on the groups making direct and the most extensive use of private funding for Smith's activities. Most of his business interests around the world are not listed in his name, so you will have to play your 'A' game."

"I have no doubt!"

Asha smiled. "I love your confidence. Let's first focus on the global banking system to trace the wire transfers around the world."

"Will do."

"Anyway, what we hope to accomplish is for you to infiltrate Smith's corporation and begin short-selling legitimate activities so investors that it will lead to expectations of the company's share price falling in the future. They should start selling all of their shares."

"Wait, you mean like that old movie, *Trading Places*?"

"Well, like that. The investors must cover the sale either by delivering some of their already owned shares to the buyer or by purchasing additional shares. They would buy at a lower price and then deliver to the buyer. We can discover those entities and shut them all down, causing them, along with Smith, to become bankrupt!"

"This is sounding like more fun than ever!"

"I am a little worried about the money transfers that occur outside the bank wires. A couple of groups use methods to repatriate funds through gold purchases."

"We can still cut off their money as well."

"How?"

"I think I can infiltrate and monitor the informal money transfer networks by determining who is safeguarding Smith's fortune. Then, I can either freeze or disrupt those assets. If I do a constructive model of relationship mapping, I can determine complex corporate structures. We can trace and identify all transactions from its origin through destination and then take action to fix and liquidate these assets."

"I knew I chose you for a reason!"

"Can I get some sleep now? Please?"

Asha laughed. "Of course. You deserve it. Goodnight."

Asha walked to the small café at the end of the Frankfurt train station and ordered an espresso. The midway stop would last forty minutes. Finding a round table just outside the entrance, she watched a six-foot, two-inch man wearing a black leather jacket walk up to the counter and order a cappuccino. After receiving his brew, he took a separate table near Asha.

"Where are your wheels?"

She pointed towards the train with her head. "You're looking at them."

"Yes, motorcycles can be quite dangerous. There was this person, back in Nice. He died of blunt force trauma to his head. It was a fatal basilar skull fracture on impact."

Asha turned pale as she gulped her espresso. "Who was he?"

"You mean, what was he?"

"What?"

"Yes, what, not who."

"I'm not following you."

"The thing you destroyed was an android."

"An android? One of Smith's?"

"No. A government model."

"Whose?"

"Not sure yet, but French? By the way, be careful with your friend."

"Who, Jericha?"

"No, Amanda. She has been rebuilt after her near fatality in Afghanistan. Almost like the Robocop."

"You are not telling me anything I don't already know. Besides, did you forget about me?"

"Oh? Did you know who she works for?"

"Yes, she's in the Secret Service."

"That's her cover title. But, like you, she answers to the president and is part of a top-secret inner agency within the NSA."

Asha looked around, making sure nobody was in earshot. "I have to go now. You should enjoy these innovative word search puzzles—pay attention to the challenging ones on pages 10 and 17."

"Thank you. I love doing those. Stay connected."

"Ciao."

"Remember what I said."

"What?"

"Be careful."

"You have my six, right?"

Chris smiled. "You betcha."

Asha returned to the train and entered her compartment. Upon entering, she gasped in horror when noticing her empty bed. She slid open the door to the bathroom. "Jericha?"

Running out of the room to the side hall, Asha moved to the dining lounge. When she burst through the door, the lounge was empty. "Dear God!"

She turned to rush back to the room and bumped into the attendant. "Oh, I'm sorry. Please forgive me! Have you seen my friend?"

"Yes, I have. She left about ten minutes after you went outside. She went with a gentleman who told her that you needed to speak with her."

"My God! Where did they go? I did not see them in the station!"

"I'm not sure, madame, but he led her towards the back of the station."

Asha took off running.

"Madame, the train will leave in ten minutes!" he yelled as she disappeared out the door.

"JERICHA? JERICHA, can you hear me?" Asha ran towards the back of the train, looking both through the train windows and across the tracks to the other stationary trains. She saw nothing out of the ordinary. Looking at the DT on her wrist, she pushed a button and watched the moving green dot. "That's gotta be her," she mumbled to herself.

Just then, the train's engine roared to life and the attendant leaned out the door to her car. "Madame, we are leaving now! Please hurry and get inside!"

Making a hurried decision, Asha jumped onto the train, ran into her room, gathered all the equipment, stuffed the items in her large rucksack and ran back towards the door. "Wait, madame, what are you doing?"

"Sorry! I must say goodbye," she answered as she timed her jump onto the platform from the slow-moving train. She was able to maintain her balance without tumbling, so she looked at her wrist again. "Not far! Hurry, Asha!" she told herself. She sprinted towards the back of the station, hoping nobody noticed her faster-than-human speed. Coming to the jumbled tracks stretched beyond the station into a dawning sky, she yelled, "JERICHA?"

The green dot was still twenty meters away. Asha removed her rucksack and crept towards the signaled location. The tall grass opened to a side road, but there was no sign of anyone. Then she spotted the DT wristwatch—lying on the ground.

Looking up into the sky, Asha prayed, "Oh, Jesus! Don't let anything happen to her, PLEASE!"

Sudden rustling behind her caused Asha to dive for cover, flattening herself on the ground. "Asha? Asha, are you here? It's me, Chris."

Recognizing his voice, she revealed herself. "It's Jericha. She's gone!"

"What happened? I saw you jump off the train and run this way. What's going on, Asha?"

"Chris, can you and your connections look for her here in Frankfurt? I need to find a way to Berlin…now!"

"Okay, any leads?"

"Here, take this picture of her to show your connections. Trace anyone or anything to do with Smith Robotics, Inc."

"What are you going to do in Berlin?"

"Do my best to get inside."

"Wait, what is that supposed to mean? Asha?"

"Please! Just find Jericha, okay? I have to continue with the mission."

"Look at me."

Asha looked up into Chris's eyes. He moved to wipe away a tear streaming down her cheek. "The last time I saw you like this; you were beaten up in a shack."

"Please don't remind me."

"I am worried about you, that I won't be able to be there when you need me."

"God has me covered."

"We'll look for Jericha. You be careful. Please!"

Asha shook her head. "I will. Promise."

"Come on, we'll get you on one of the day commutes to Berlin."

Asha shook her head again. "Chris?"

"What is it, Ash?"

"Thank you," she said before wrapping her arms around him. "Could you please just hold me?"

Chris did not answer but responded by holding her against him. She allowed his embrace to linger for half a minute before she pulled away. Then she looked up at him and said, "I have to make a phone call now. I'll catch up with you at the ticket counter."

"Alright, Asha. Let me take your ruck."

She nodded her approval as he grabbed her rucksack and walked back towards the main station. "I'll be right behind you," she added.

There was no answer at the other end of her attempts to call Amanda. None of the three devices was able to establish communications. "Come on, Amanda, now's not the time to sleep. Please wake up!" She tried again on all three devices, the primary and both backups. Still, there was no answer. Putting her mobiles away, Asha walked towards the main station until she caught up with Chris.

"You're in luck, Asha. A train leaves for Berlin in an hour."

"Something's wrong!"

"You think? You're missing one of your team members."

"No, something's not right with my other team member…Amanda."

Chris looked at her with deep concern. "The one I told you is with the NSA? What happened?"

"She's not answering any of our primary or backup comms."

"Maybe you better abort this mission, Asha."

"I can't!"

"I'm serious!"

"So am I, Chris! I can't!"

"At least let me go with you to Berlin."

"No! You have to find Jericha, remember?"

"I have some guys here who can track her down."

Asha thought for a moment, tempted by the proposition. "No, this mission has already been compromised, and the less operators, the better my chances. Please, Chris. Find Jericha. I need to do this, okay?"

Chris nodded and waited until she purchased her ticket. "Be careful Asha. Contact me as soon as you arrive. I will see what we can do here. I'll let you know."

Asha looked down. "Thanks again, Chris. I'll call you."

"Asha. Look at me."

She looked up, back into his eyes.

"You have not lost yet. This is not your fault. The mission is still in front of you. I'm here for you, just stay in touch."

"I must go now. I'll call you."

"You better! I mean it!"

TWENTY – Lady of the Night

The sun was bright over the capital city of Germany when the commuter train stopped at the Hauptbahnhof. Berlin was Germany's largest city and considered by many as the cultural capital of all Europe. The twelve boroughs grouped into six districts offered plenty of museums, shops, and palaces, as well as an active nightlife.

Asha departed the train and walked to the front of the station to hail a taxi. "Bitte nehmen sie mich hier," she said while handing the driver a piece of notebook paper.

The taxi driver nodded his head. "Sicher," he responded before walking around back to open his trunk for Asha's bag.

"Ich werde dies halten mit mir, dankethe." *I will hold this one with me.*

The driver shrugged his shoulders, got back in the driver seat, and headed towards East Berlin. The rush hour traffic had started, so the trip took about thirty minutes. When the taxi pulled up to the building displaying the address, he turned and asked Asha, "Sind sie sicher, dass dies der richtige ort ist?"

Asha handed him some Euros. "Dies ist der richtige ort. Danke."

"Vielen Dank, Frau," the driver replied with a smile.

She hesitated outside the building before entering. Although the lobby was not what she had been accustomed to in Nice, it still looked clean.

Two young girls came down the stairs, watching her. One of them uttered a sarcastic welcome to Asha. "Haben Sie keine Angst Honig sein. Man, gewöhnt sich daran." The other girl laughed.

"Well, you want a room?" the woman at the front desk asked her in English.

"Yes. Do you have one available facing the street?"

"I have one on the third floor. It will cost €50.00 per night. You want it?"

"Yes. I'll take it."

"Good. Sign here. I take the money now."

"Oh. Here," Asha said, handing her the money before stooping to sign the paper.

"Here is the key. Would you like me to take you there, or do you want to go there yourself?"

"I'll find it, thank you."

"Third floor, two doors past the elevator."

"Thanks."

Asha noticed that the two girls who passed her earlier were still standing outside. With tight clothes and bum bags strapped around their waists, they seemed ready to begin their workday. Walking up to them, she asked, "Wohin gehst du, um Ihre Kleidung zu bekommen?"

"Your German is good...for an American," one of them answered in an English accent. "Where did you learn it?"

"I have American written all over me?"

"Not too bad. We heard you talk to Janet, the lady at the desk, in English."

"I see. My name is Asha."

"My name is Boyka, but many call me Bouncy."

"Bouncy?"

"Yes," Boyka answered, giggling.

The other girl spoke up. "My name is Kalyna, but I have a nickname too. It is Groan."

"Groan?"

"Yes, GROAN!" the second girl chimed in—adding a groan for emphasis. The two prostitutes erupted in laughter.

Asha chuckled at their humor. "Where are you two from?"

"Now? Everywhere. Nowhere."

"Your home country?"

"We're both from the Ukraine," Boyka answered.

"I've been there before."

The girls looked at her with delight. "You have been to our country? When?"

"When I was 11 years old. I was visiting my grandfather. He has a yacht on the Dnieper."

The girls looked scared. "We must go now. Do you see that place over there with the big glass window?"

Asha followed her pointed finger. "Yes."

"Get your clothes in there."

"What makes you think…?"

"Why else do you come here?"

"Okay, what do you recommend?"

"Everything in there is good," Kalyna answered, followed by another long, purring moan. Tell them that Groan sent you, and be sure to add emphasis to my name. You will get a discount."

The two girls laughed, and Boyka added, "Yes, and if you tell them your name is Aaahhhsha, they might give you something for free."

The two turned and walked down the street, laughing, leaving Asha standing and shaking her head. "They're crazy," she muttered to herself.

Going back inside and stopping at the front desk, she asked Janet, "Is there room service here?"

"Yes, of course. What can we bring you?"

"Maybe something to eat and drink?"

"No worry. You go up to your room, and I will have someone special bring it to you in half an hour."

"Uh—okay, thank you."

Asha entered the quaint room, which turned out to be nice...better than she expected. There was a small refrigerator, HDTV, and a decorative bathtub in a small, but cozy bathroom. The bed was queen-sized and covered with a red bedspread. Asha walked to the window and looked outside. Two other girls joined the two she just met. They were all standing by the roadside close to

Hackescher Markt, one of Berlin's busiest shopping and entertainment districts. *So, this is where the pipeline comes,* Asha thought.

The one-kilometer strip in the Berlin Mitte district attracted a host of gullible tourists. The Intelligence Summary from Chris pinpointed this area as a channel to the UAE and Cyber-Smith City.

She closed the curtain and sat down at the edge of her bed. Again, she tried calling Amanda from all the communication devices she carried. After twenty minutes of no response, she pulled her Bible from her pack, opened to Joshua chapter 2, and read to chapter 6. When she came to verse twenty-five, she read it aloud, "But Joshua spared Rahab the prostitute."

Asha flopped back on the bed and drifted off to sleep. The rapping on the door startled her awake. "Wer ist es?"

"It's room service," came a man's voice in English.

She peered through the small hole and saw that he had some towels and a bottle of wine in his hand.

"Janet said you could use these," he started while handing her the towels. "And this? My compliments! My way of welcoming you on your first night with us!" he said with a broad smile while handing her the bottle of wine.

Asha started to give him some money.

"No, no, no, my dear. This is my place. I own it!"

"Oh, I'm sorry. I didn't mean…"

"No apologies necessary. I am having one of our cooks prepare you something special to eat for dinner this evening, before you, well, before you go outside to visit our streets," he said with a grin.

"That is truly kind of you, thank you. I did not get your name."

"Just call me Hans. Everybody else does. You made an excellent choice to come here. Tell me, how did you hear of this place, if you don't mind me asking?"

"Oh, you know. Word of mouth."

The slick-haired man in his early forties belted out with laughter, startling Asha. "Yes, yes, I like that one! Word of mouth! Your dinner should be ready in thirty minutes. I will bring it up myself! Well, until later!"

Asha watched him leave, disappearing down the hallway, still laughing and saying, "Word of mouth, I love it!"

She shook her head and smiled. Talking to herself, she muttered, "Are you sure about all this, Asha?" Picking up her phone, she dialed Chris' number.

"Hello, Asha?"

"Hi, Chris. I'm here, and okay for now."

"Asha, I have some news, and it's not all good."

Asha stood. "What—what is it?"

"First, we followed some leads on Jericha. The trail leads to…"

"Cyber-Smith City?"

"Yes, I'm afraid so."

"Go on!"

"I did that puzzle you gave me and figured out what you were trying to tell me. The answer is yes, not just a possibility, but this was the same lead Amanda was following in conjunction with your mission."

"Wait. Homeland Security?"

"Yes!"

"What about Amanda? Tell me you know something."

"Yes…and it's not good."

"What? What is it?"

"Seems that the droid you killed was a French security droid model, and the French were able to trace its…and this is going to sound crazy, DNA back to where you met Amanda in Morocco."

"So, the authorities have her?"

"The last we were able to find out, she is in French custody."

Asha, too deep in thought, mind whirling, did not answer.

"Asha? Did you hear me?"

"Yes. Sorry."

"Asha. Stay there. I'm coming to get you."

"Nooo! Not now. This may be my only chance of getting inside."

"Well, in case you have been sleepwalking while I've been talking, your team is disintegrating!"

"But…"

"But nothing, Asha. We are coming to your location. Hold tight!"

Asha did not respond.

"Where are you?"

"Call me when you get in town," she answered before terminating the call.

Asha decided to check out the clothing store pointed out to her by the two Ukrainian girls. Stopping in front of the big pink sign that read *SweetHeartz*, she mumbled to herself, "Well, here goes."

Inside, Asha watched the few girls who were inside browsing, noting which section attracted the most customers. The more prevalent clothes were tight fitting, short skirts coming in various shades of red and white and tight-fitting tops that exposed a lot of flesh. In Berlin, the nights were still cool enough for most of the prostitutes to sport a lightweight jacket. This suited Asha the most, both for the semi-modest appearance and for concealing a small handgun.

Something else caught Asha's attention, though she did not make it obvious, as she selected the clothing she would don for the evening. A blonde-haired female, who came in five minutes after she did, seemed too interested in her movements. Asha decided the timing was good to make her purchase and exit back to the hotel.

"Wird dies alles sein?"

Asha grabbed a few items at the register and said, "Bitte fugen Sie diese."

Rather than going outside, Asha went to the restroom and changed into her new clothes. After putting on a pair of sunglasses, she exited and decided to walk in the opposite direction of the hotel and wait until the blonde-haired girl emerged from the store. When she did, two minutes after Asha departed, without any shopping bags, Asha turned and walked towards GroBer Tiergarten Park. The girl followed. Whenever Asha picked up the pace, the blonde-haired person did likewise.

She discounted the numerous drones flying overhead, which was following a routine pattern of surveillance. Asha sat down at a nearby café table and acted as if nothing was amiss. Within seconds, she noticed that the young woman stopped in the tree's shadows. Although Asha did not look her way, she sensed the girl was watching.

Asha's glistening brown eyes focused on the blonde-haired woman while a swooping overhead drone distracted her attention. In that moment, the girl began running towards her. Asha stood up and wondered whether she should stand and fight or run like the devil.

Before making that decision, a blinding flash of light and ear-splitting bang led to a forceful wave that sent Asha across the sidewalk. Landing on the concrete pavement, she lay motionless. A minute went by when she pushed herself up with an elbow and gazed towards the sky, now engulfed by a black mushroom cloud rising above her.

Dazed and semi-conscious, Asha continued to lift herself, reaching out to anything she could find, as pieces of flesh and shreds of blood-soaked clothing mingled with other debris fell around her. Tiny pieces of glass landed like drops of rain with tinkling sounds. Instinctively, she curled into a ball while holding her other hand over her head. A crude smell lingered in the air, causing her to heave and choke.

Asha stopped hearing things hit the ground, so she pushed herself up again, first to her knees, and then to a full standing position. The tranquil moment turned into a grisly nightmare with one quick detonation of a bomb.

Holding her hands out in front of her, Asha turned them over, trying to focus on each finger. Everything was intact. She looked down at her legs and observed trickles of blood running from both knees, which took the brunt of the landing.

Chaos ensued in all directions around her. The screams were deafening and heart-wrenching sobs from those bent over a dying or dead loved one. A roaring humming sound whistled above her, causing Asha to look skyward again, in time to see two drones hover over the scene. Three other drones arrived just before the wailing sirens in the distance grew louder.

I must vacate—now!

Glass littered the ground between her and her Beacons, separated during the blast force. One of them was five meters to her left, and the other was ten meters beyond the first one. Asha would have no choice but to gather them the best she could, since sharp objects surrounded her in every direction.

She took small, careful steps towards her nearest shoe, maneuvering through the shattered glass—wincing with each step. The painstaking task left a small trail of blood behind her. Reaching the first shoe, she placed it on her blood-soaked foot and hopped to the other one, grunting in pain with each contact on pavement. After putting on her other shoe, she stopped to survey the carnage around her. *The case for wearing my boots*, she thought.

A smoking crater was located at the area below the tree where the girl once stood, and the shredded debris hung from the surrounding tree branches. The screaming continued, and sirens from all types of emergency vehicles grew louder from every direction. Before hurrying to the hotel, Asha looked around her immediate vicinity to see if she could assist anyone in need. Everybody she saw was either already dead or being dealt with by another, so she hurried the best she could, with glass in her feet, towards the hotel. Asha surmised it would take ten minutes for the walk back.

On her way, she stopped long enough to look back at the scene, now swarmed with emergency personnel, then looked up at the sky. "Thank you, Lord! Thank you for protecting me." Then she continued back to the hotel, wondering, *If I was the target, why did the bomb go off so soon?*

Arriving back to her hotel, Asha limped to the elevator.

"My dear child, are you all right? What happened?" The owner asked, his face paler than she remembered.

"Yes, I am fine. There was a bomb by the park."

"Dear God! Come; let me help you to your room!"

"Thank you. I will be okay."

The man hesitated, then ran to the entrance, Janet right behind him, as they both went outside for a closer look. Asha went on, desiring to clean up and check out as fast as she could.

Sliding the keycard across her door, she entered and observed her safety measure, indicating whether anyone had trespassed in her absence. There were no signs of intrusion.

Asha threw off her clothes and limped to the bathtub, leaving a slight trail of red splotches and partial footprints on the carpet. This was the least of her concern. Sitting at the back edge of the tub, she swung her feet into the rising lukewarm water pouring from the spout. The clear liquid changed to a light pinkish color, but it was not long before it regained a more bluish tint, matching the color of the ceramic.

Rubbing the bottom of her feet gently, Asha tried to wash away all the tiny pieces of glass. Convinced that her skin was clear of foreign particles, she allowed the water to drain, altered her feet over the tile and onto a padded towel lying on the floor. After moving the towel across the bottom of her feet to remove whatever might be left over, she walked to the linen closet and grabbed a white cotton blouse. Then she decided to try on the new pair of shorts she had just purchased, which fit exactly right around her waist but were at least eight inches above her knees. *Good grief,* she thought after looking at herself in the mirror. *Why even bother?*

Walking towards her bed, she sat at the foot, backwards onto the mattress. Then she closed her eyes. *Okay, think, Asha, think.*

Past scenes flooded her mind, scenes that merged into a colored kaleidoscope maze. The maze formed into a spinning circle, winding towards an abrupt splash of white light that lit her semi-conscious state. Startled, she sat up with a whimper. The room was quiet. Outside, she could still hear the distant clatter of sirens and the humming drones.

"Oh, Dad," she cried aloud, "what would you do in this situation? You would know."

Asha jumped up, gathered her traveling clothes along with her other gear, and headed for the door, dismissing any thoughts of imminent threats.

Pausing at the mirror, Asha examined herself and realized that she still had on the tight shorts. "Oh, pooh," she exclaimed. Her dark hair caught the outer edge of each eyebrow before her strands hung loose over her shoulders. Her intense brown eyes stared back at her, emitting an elevated look of concern, more tense than when she saw herself before the past forty-eight hours. "No time now."

She placed a light denim jacket on and grabbed her small .25 Beretta automatic. After extracting the clip, she left a single round in the barrel, and then placed the lever on safe before sticking the weapon inside a pocket she designed in the jacket's interior lining.

Looking around the room once more, she walked to the front door and looked through the tiny glass hole before opening it.

Stepping outside into the corridor, everything was clear. Her plan was to hail a taxi to the airport and book a flight to the UAE and hope for the best. Asha did not intend to stay around Berlin any longer…somebody had wanted her dead.

When the elevator door opened, a six-foot, five-inch, black-haired man stepped out in front of her. She did not recognize him. Noting his intense grey-blue eyes never left hers, she reached for her gun— but it was too late.

TWENTY-ONE - Captured

Asha emerged from a terrible dream; her hands tied together behind her on the outside of a hard wooden chair. She tried with effort to wriggle them free, but whoever fastened them did so with precision and strength. Her bare feet were secured together in front of her as complete darkness covered her eyes.

Feeling a cloth wrapped around her forehead and tied to the back, a sense of relief came when she realized that the lack of visual was due to a blindfold rather than any physical damage to her eyes.

Asha's instinct was to fight, but since she had no idea what was surrounding her, she took advantage of her mouth being free from obstruction. "Hello? Anyone here?"

The nightmarish thoughts of her training returned, and she began to panic. "Who is here?"

A shoulder-length, brunette-haired woman with glistening brown, almond shaped eyes stood in front of her. The girl nodded to the six-foot, five-inch muscle-bound man standing behind the chair, who proceeded to remove the rag covering Ashas eyes.

"Hello, Asha."

Trying to focus her eyes, she answered, "Who are you, and what do you want?"

The girl smiled. "Please promise me you will cooperate, and I'll untie your hands."

Asha took in her surroundings. "Why should I promise you anything?" she demanded while struggling to get free.

"You are assessing your situation. Smart girl. There is no way to escape. We mean you no harm. I want to help you. You must trust me."

Looking straight into the girl's eyes, Asha answered defiantly, "I trust no one. You cannot help me, and I will not help you."

The girl looked up at the man behind Asha and turned her head back and forth sideways, then stepped closer to Asha. Kneeling, she moved her face to within inches of Asha. "You look a lot like your father."

"Wha-what do you know about my father? Where is he? What did you do with him?"

The girl smiled. "Your father, and mother for that matter, are fine, still in India, I believe, yes?"

"What did you do to them, you witch? I will kill you if -"

"Please calm down, Asha. I would never do anything to hurt your parents. We need your help."

"They are, okay? Why should I believe you? Who are you?"

Sensing her defiance subsiding, the girl nodded to the muscular man behind the chair, who proceeded to untie her hands. When he came around to release the binding around her feet, he glanced at Asha sternly before proceeding to untie the cord. Standing between the two women, he crossed his arms, watching Asha the whole time. The man looked to be in his late thirties, but his leathery appearance indicated that he spent much of his life outdoors. He did not smile.

"Please excuse Stojan, he doesn't say much."

Asha cast a sideways glance at him as she rubbed her hands and then her feet, trying to rush circulation back into her extremities. "Where are my shoes?

"I have them here. Are you thirsty? I have some water if you would like some."

Asha received the glass of water, looked in it for a second, and looked back at the girl standing in front of her.

"It's okay." The woman took a sip and handed it back to Asha, who downed the clear liquid in one gulp.

Handing back the empty glass, Asha said, "Could I have some more, please?"

The girl chuckled. "As I was saying, we need your help."

"What kind of help? You still haven't told me who you are!"

"Eleven years ago, your father was sent on a mission to Iraq. He brought back a young girl. Mariam, yes?"

Asha looked at her.

"He was not able to tell you everything about that mission because it was top secret. Much of it had to do with me."

"You?"

"Yes, me. I played the role of your father's wife. Together, we had to rescue Mariam as a couple or else jeopardize the whole operation. Your dad would know me by the name Lyna."

Asha eyed her with mistrust. "And your real name?"

"I go by four different ones, depending on the situation. It does not matter. What matters is that our nation is in trouble, and we need your help."

"Your nation? Which one?"

"Our nations. All of them!"

Asha continued to study the pretty woman, who looked to be near forty. You still have not told me for whom you work."

"Like I said before, it does not matter who I work for…"

"It does to me!" Asha snapped.

"The explosion near your hotel. Do you know who that girl was, the one who targeted you?"

Asha's mind switched to a defensive mode at the mention of the bomb. "What do you know about that?"

"We know the girl was targeting you, and if we had not intervened, you would not be alive right now."

"Intervened? How?"

"We forced a premature triggering device to explode before the assassin could get too close to you."

"Assassin? Well, she was close enough!"

"You are here, are you not?"

"Okay. Let's say you want to help me. Where are my team members? Do you even know about them?"

"Amanda and Jericha Hyatt…"

"Where are they?"

"Jericha is in Cyber-Smith City."

"Amanda? What about her?"

"Whereabouts unknown." Her answer prompted Asha to jump from her chair. The muscular man stepped towards her. Asha had him lying on the ground in seconds, yelling in pain. The overhead lights flicked on brightly.

"Enough of this," came a voice from a man in a business suit. Two AK-47-wielding guards flanked him on either side. Their weapons pointed at Asha.

"See, I told you so," Lyna stated. "She is much like her father and is a weapon herself."

The sturdy, gray-haired man with piercing blue eyes got up from his desk and emerged from the shadows, his two guards following him. The man spoke in Russian and told the guards to help Stojan, who was moaning and trying with difficulty to rise from the floor. The guards moved to aid their fallen comrade and were horrified to see that Stojans leg bent in an awkward position below the knee.

Coming closer to where Asha was still standing, the man continued in Russian. "Asha, moy rebenok. Eto ya. Vash dedushka."

"Grandpa? Grandpa? Is—is that you?

Viktor Tamarov walked up to his granddaughter and stopped in front of her. Smiling, he continued. "You have grown up to be a beautiful woman, my child."

"Grandpa?" Asha asked again. "It—it is you?"

"Of course. As you once told me when you were much younger, and we were on the boat. Really."

They both took a step closer towards each other, looking into the other's eyes. "You still have your grandmother's eyes," Viktor said in fond remembrance of his Tajik bride.

Asha lunged at him with an emotional hug, causing the bodyguards to move towards Asha until Viktor held up his hand while receiving her embrace. "Oh, Grandpa! It has been so long!"

"Too long, my child, too long."

They held each other for half a minute or so before Asha blurted, "Grandpa, what is going on? Please tell me!"

He nodded his head and looked at his guards. "Pereyti zabotitsya o Stojan. Ubedites chto on poluchayet sootvetstvuyushcheye lecheniye!"

Looking at the girl who introduced herself as Lyna, Viktor said, "Please. Join us."

She nodded in agreement, and the two women followed Viktor through a side door into a plush office. "Make yourself at home, ladies." The room began filling with servants, some bringing tea, others food, and one who brought a folder. Once Viktor was satisfied with everything, he waited for the room to clear, leaving him, Asha, and Lyna.

"Are you hungry or thirsty, my dear?"

"Both," Asha answered.

"Help yourself to some tea and food. We have some bread, meat, and cheeses, as well as some fruit."

"Thank you, Grandpa."

He smiled. "My pleasure, dear one, my pleasure."

Looking at Lyna, he offered the same choices.

"I am fine, thank you."

"Not even some tea?"

Lyna watched Asha put together a plate. "Sure, why not?"

Asha wasted little time stuffing the food into her mouth and washing it down with hot tea. "Grandpa, please tell me what you know about Amanda and Jericha!"

"Very well. Amanda Hyatt works for the NSA, at the top level. Even before she met you, she was on a Top Secret and specific mission to trace, or weed out, top level agency officials within your own government who have been collaborating with Smith Robotics, Inc."

"More than one official?"

"Our sources indicate at least five, if not more."

"So, Amanda was destined to be on my team all along?"

"Your president figured you would draw a logical conclusion, which you did."

"And Jericha?"

"Everything she told you is true. She was not aware of any other agenda."

"Are they safe? Are they okay?"

Lyna answered, "Our people have traced Jericha to Cyber-Smith City, where, for the moment, she is alive."

"Your people? You are Russian?"

Lyna laughed. "Sometimes."

"You are not going to tell me, then?"

"When you need to know, you will. Right now, the most important thing is to get inside Cyber-Smith City and find her and those you were sent to rescue and bring them home."

"Agreed…but there is more. I…" She stopped and looked at her grandfather. The thought flashed through her mind, *If I cannot trust my own grandfather, whom could I trust?* "I am also assigned to destroy Smith and his operation."

Viktor responded, "We have been aware of this."

Asha wondered how her grandfather, and whoever this woman was, could know such top-level information. "What do you know?"

Lyna spoke. "We know that you, Amanda, and Jericha planned and trained together and then were sent to specialized locations for specifics."

"How could you know this?"

"Asha, right now, this is not the most important matter. Please listen to Lyna, just for a moment."

Asha started to say something but backed down. "Okay, Grandpa."

Lyna continued. "Members of your government agencies at prominent levels have sent out teams to stop your mission. Because of their official status, they can collaborate with foreign agencies. French authorities took Amanda from the villa where you left her. We swept through the complex that night after the authorities were finished and found nothing."

"She had our specialized equipment!"

The French believed that they were handing her back over to the NSA. The NSA is disavowing this claim.

"Dear God! I led them right to her!"

TWENTY-TWO - Revelation

"What a fool I am!"

"There's no way you could have known about their security droid. If in imminent danger, these particular models are designed to release a traceable DNA onto anyone they come into physical contact with."

Asha looked distraught. "And Jericha? Somebody picked up her trail in Paris!"

"Yes, our sources indicate that at least one of those high-level officials is from the American Homeland Security Department."

"I think I know who!"

"Have you noticed that every time you met with your army contact friend, something goes wrong?"

Asha jumped up, deep in thought. "How did…never mind. Wait a minute. Every time I contacted…"

"You can say his name, Sergeant First Class Short. We know…"

Asha sat down without saying anything more.

Viktor interjected, "We are not blaming him personally, Asha, but we believe he is receiving much of his information through the chain of command, a chain that starts with orders from the Department of the Army and possibly within his own Special Forces Group."

Asha sat with her head down in her hands, not knowing what to say.

"Asha, we had to get you before your own people did. Please believe this. We also had to do so without leaving any traces—taking you off the grid, so-to-speak."

She nodded her understanding, letting the words sink into her mind. "You said I could help you save our countries. How? What is Smith up to? What is his plan?

"Our inside source has confirmed that particular humans are being cloned, or as Smith calls it, replicated, into humanoids that will be released back to their original settings or in the general public with the intent to rule this planet."

"My God! Why would Smith do such a thing?"

"Your father would have said the same," Lyna replied, "but it is Smith who is playing God."

"The young girls? Nicole? How—how?"

"What is their role? A mixture of high-level madness and personal perverted pleasure on the part of leading officials within the Homeland Security Department."

"I—I just cannot believe this!"

"It is true, my love," Viktor interjected. "We have evidence from our insider."

"Your insider. Who is he, or she?"

"We cannot divulge this information at this time. You must understand the sensitive nature of this whole operation."

"But how can I help—if I am not made aware of your inside connection?"

"You will know at the precise moment when it is critical that you need to know."

Asha stood and ran her hands through her hair. "I just cannot conceive any of this right now. What can I do?"

"We have a plan that can get you inside, all the way to the top," Lyna said.

"And it will not involve you playing any part of a prostitute!" Viktor added sternly.

"I—I could not think of another way. Besides, I wasn't going to go through with it."

"It is okay. We know nothing happened. Lyna has been working on this for a period."

"Okay."

"I have been invited as a special guest by Mr. Stan Smith himself. He accepted my request as Dr. Abigail Assaf of Tshai Institute, located in Kiev, Ukraine."

"There is such a place?"

"Government-controlled, but I am not really Dr. Assaf. I have been invited as an anthropomorphist, the study…"

"…of robots on society and the human relationship."

"Yes. You would come as my protégé…my own humanoid creation."

Asha started to laugh. "What? Do you know about me too? Are you crazy?"

"Please, my darling Asha. You must not laugh. We are profoundly serious about this matter."

"I am sorry, Grandpa. It is just irrational to think about this."

"Asha, I would not ask you to be a part of this if I did not believe it would work. I would never want to see any harm come to you in any way…ever!"

"I know, Grandpa. I can make it work."

"That's what we thought. We would be able to get an inside look at Smith's operation, something nobody has been able to do. This is our best opportunity."

"And then? Once the two of us are inside, what is the plan?"

"Our mission is much like yours, the destruction of Smith Robotics, Inc. As we mentioned before, we have an insider who has been in-depth for three years. There are two special operation teams on standby for coordinated infiltration, rescue, demolition, and exfiltration."

"These teams, any of them American?"

"No. Your president did not want to jeopardize your operation, and he did not know who he could trust at this time."

"Can I ask where these teams are from? What country they represent?"

Lyna looked at Viktor, who nodded his approval. "It is a combined force of Spetsnaz and Sayeret."

"The Israeli Special Forces? You— you are?"

Lyna cut her off. "Yes. I work for the Mossad."

Everything Asha heard in this room was overwhelming, but she had no reason to doubt her grandfather, nor a woman who claimed to have played the role of her father's wife. "When do we leave?" Asha said eagerly.

"As a matter of fact, our flight into Smithsport is tomorrow morning."

Looking at her grandfather, Asha wanted affirmation. "Grandpa?"

"Yes, my dear?"

"I have one request to make."

"I am listening."

"No matter what happens to me, I need Jericha alive. I need her to complete the electronic demolition of Smith's network infrastructure."

Viktor looked at Lyna, then got up, walked over to Asha, and gave her another emotional embrace. "My dear one. I am confident that everything will be all right and that your mission will be a success. You are working with the best, and I will add, you are also the best! I believe this, right here," he said, pointing to his heart.

ᵚ

Chris Short, along with two team members, went inside Asha's room. Janet had let them inside, telling them, "I did not see her leave."

"But she did come back here after the bomb?" Chris asked her.

"Yes, we spoke. She was limping a little. We wanted to help her, but she said she was okay."

"And you didn't see anybody else around…anybody strange?"

"No, we did not see…"

Suddenly, the door flung open and four masked people dressed completely in black burst into the room, each holding an XM-10 assault rifle. A female voice screamed in German, "Niemand bewegen!" Chris and his team lifted their hands high. "Wer bist du!"

Chris spoke up. "Ich bin ein amerikanischer Soldat. Wir sind auf der Suche nach einem anderen Mitglied."

The leader motioned with her head while the three others with rifles searched Chris and his team. Then she looked at Janet and said, "Raus hier!"

She ran out the door in haste. The assault team brought the items that they found to the leader. She examined their handguns, looked at the communication devices and the cell phone history. She began removing her mask and said in English, "Stand down."

The three members with weapons complied. Chris and his team looked at the leader as she removed her cover.

"You are Chris Short?"

"Who wants to know?"

"I am Amanda."

"What? Asha thought you were captured!"

"So do many others. This is good. We will retain the element of surprise. Right now, we all must disappear from this location. You, my friend, are being tagged."

"By whom?"

"Our own people. I had to go deeper with my cover once we realized that Asha's life, and our mission, was in jeopardy. This became apparent in Nice."

"My people? Who do you work for anyway?"

"The NSA. Now, if you are finished asking questions, let's move, or do you already have an exfiltration plan?"

Chris looked at his two friends. "We'll follow you!"

"Let's go!"

TWENTY-THREE – Cyber City, Dubai

An ashen sky gave way to streaks of magenta and lilac across Cyber-Smith City when Asha and Lyna arrived by a private chartered aircraft. Moving from the jet to an awaiting hovercraft, the two women walked through fields of grass that grew in elevated honeycomb patterns.

Lyna held credentials as Dr. Abigail Assaf of Tshai Institute, holding the credentials of Critically Adaptive trans-Disciplinary Engineering, Mathematics, Informatics, & Arts. Her assistant and protégé, Asha, went by the name Hannah Jordan.

In Cyber-Smith City, social stratification was based on each person's skills in problem-solving, adaptive learning, their ability to construct and shape materials, and to write and decipher code. The explanation given by Stan Smith's spokesperson, Stella Light, to any outside inquiries concerning the many young women seen throughout the city was the fact that they were all students, selected for their intellect.

The other exception allowed contractors for the purpose of expanding building sites and artists to express the ideals of individual freedom and creativity. The new buildings, framed and labeled as Pads, were the basis of innovated interconnected corridors that hovered above basic streets. Most all the young girls and contractors were separated in two principal areas in square detached houses surrounding Smith's headquarters in the center of Cyber-Smith City.

Stan Smith began several developments with the goal of having over a billion network connectivity items planned for smart cities by 2025. Focusing on recent technologies, such as the Internet of Things (IoT), 3D printing, augmented reality and artificial intelligence, he grew individuals and businesses in similar fashion that saw Google flourish in 2016.

Taking advantage of the open public data collected from connected things created infrastructure benefits for Smith, benefits that included energy, water network efficiency, relief of traffic congestion, improvements to city facilities, and humanoid robots. In his so-called smart buildings, sensors detected and identified all people that ever entered any of his facilities. This information fed into his office network center and gave him the upper hand in negotiations and contracts over the highest competitors.

Smith's process of reducing urban management triggered cities to become environmental centers of excellence. His firm drove real-time change behavior through analytics, new communications, and social media apps. His engineers developed sustainable science solutions for complex problems with social, economic, and environmental elements, reaching from local to global scales. By his design thinking, his team synthesized information from distinct sources to arrive at design concepts that helped solve advanced human aspirations in the form of artificial intelligence.

Cyber-Smith City was the new hub for investments in high-tech clusters and recruiting research-intensive companies. It became the home to several companies, such as Intel, Honeywell, and Orbital Sciences. A rising economic technology growth resulted in increased jobs making life in Cyber-Smith City a mini paradise, except for the exploited.

Repeated interactions between research teams and stakeholders led to high-level relationships throughout the world. Smith's team vetted different sets of scenario elements through interviews and workshops that included experts in high-risk insurance, venture capital, media, urban economic development, regulations, patent law and technology transfer, nanoscale science and engineering, and sustainability challenges.

Smith Robotics, Inc., leveraged the fact that citizens hoped to become wealthy and famous entrepreneurs. He sought government-funded agencies focusing on small business research grants to privatize and market technologies created in universities and federal labs. By outsourcing numerous small businesses loyal to his program, he was able to attract national conferences, researchers, budding entrepreneurs, and program managers.

336 | SCOTT MEEHAN

Rays of sunlight pierced Nicole's bed. The windows tinting melted away as the night's sky transformed into a grayish-purple aurora in anticipation of morning. In addition to her lack of freedom and living in a place against her will, she faced another day of uncertainty; another day away from her home; another day away from her family. It had been two months since her arrival, and although she abhorred her life situation, she avoided the enforcement to appease a strange man; unlike the others, she knew who she was dealing with. The aroma of freshly brewed coffee greeted her when Stella brought in her food tray. She grabbed the brew first and sipped it cautiously.

"Today will be your lucky day, my child."

Nicole choked on her coffee. "My lucky day? I can go home?"

"No, dear, you cannot go home. Not yet anyway. You are needed for something particularly important. It is exceedingly high level, in fact."

Nicole could not hide the fearful look in her eyes. "What—what do you mean?

"You will find out soon enough, but for now, please eat your breakfast. The man who will visit you today is a high government official. He is from America. He will take you home, who knows?"

Nicole lost her appetite. With emotions charged, she was afraid of the inevitable agonizing day she hoped would never come. On the other hand, she held a glimmer of hope that an American official could rescue her and Makeala. Sensing that there might be a slight glimmer of hope, Nicole decided to eat. "Do you know him?"

"He's been here before. Mr. Smith treats him like a particularly important leader."

"And he's from America?"

"Yes, I believe so. I will go now and come back for your tray in an hour."

"Wait! When will he come?"

"Sometime today. I do not know." Stella, who was one of the servant droids, left the room, locking the door behind her from the outside.

Nicole watched her close the door, wondering who would appear next whenever it opened. *I hope I can see Makeala this morning before the visit*, she thought to herself. The two, separated and given their own rooms, were together once Makeala recovered from whatever ordeal she had experienced, one that she herself could not explain to Nicole since she was in an unconscious state.

The market price of solar had never quite caught up with the decreasing price of nuclear, coal, and natural gas. There were hundreds of reasons due to technology and politics for the lack of solar energy taking off as the new world's energy source. A large part of the problem stemmed from massive droughts across many regions, including the western United States. As a result, water, rather than the century old oil, became the new battleground between the aristocratic nations and the proletariat countries.

Mission-oriented government agencies, like the Department of Defense, Department of Homeland Security, and the National Institutes of Health, all collaborated with private contractors to create novel technological solutions to social problems. Cyber-Smith City was an experimental city, and with the cooperation with the UAE government, construction began in 2018 thirty miles from Dubai.

Successful accomplishment relied upon historic feats of science and engineering, and identifiable threats. Leaders from the security agencies led to the containment of threats and mitigated many stressors of urban life, the economy, and environment. By 2024, Smith relied on the latest humanoid technology to build a large security network throughout the city.

ﻼﻚ

Asha awakened to the morning rays gently easing their way through the blinds in her plush hotel room at the Grand Plaza. The Desert Sunrise, programmed into the Home Intelligence System, synchronized every second with all management systems within Cyber-Smith City.

Those who wished to become citizens of Cyber-Smith City were vetted through an extensive screening process, and if accepted into resident status, children had to be encoded with their Social Security numbers embedded within eighty-one discrete codons using synthetic G-A-C-T sequences.

As Asha peeked through the blinds, she whispered, "This is the day the Lord has made. I will rejoice and be glad in it," before walking to the bathroom to depress her hands in a semi-solid gel that filled the sink monitoring station. The system massaged her hands, scrubbed her skin, and then applied a nail polish pattern. What Asha did not know was that the scrubbing segment of the massage had painlessly extracted dead skin cells that gathered in a vacuum tube leading to the security headquarters, set up by Interpol. By analyzing these cells, her identity would be discovered within 24-48 hours.

Dark clouds gave way to the morning's rays. Dr. Ernest Gray awakened to the pungent aroma of creosote oils mixed with ozone—a smell of rain and the promise of wildflowers in the desert. He opened the windows to let in some light and fresh air while listening to the hushed tones of others, followed by laughter.

Working habitually late hours at the Center for Cytogenetic research, Dr. Gray looked forward to giving a tour to a new team of visiting researchers. He was an elite member of the Collective of Researchers and Entrepreneurs, otherwise known as CORE, which was comprised of financiers, lawyers, citizens, scientists, engineers, city water planners, Cybernetic engineers, and rotating educators from the high school and college level.

The CORE department of Smith's empire collaborated with civic organizations and scientific researchers to discover root causes of a wide variety of persistent challenges. Strategic plans focused on improving symptoms, while targeting the underlying causes. The science policy agenda addressed societal challenges where risk mitigation relied on citizen buy-in to maintain the city infrastructure.

Children and adults of all ages learn from a personalized, skills-based education system based on a model that supported a competitive, creative population attuned to individual rewards. Cyber-Smith City, in conjunction with government agencies, posted daily challenges on challenge boards with individuals advancing based on their ability to solve more extraordinary problems.

Corporate Research and Development (R&D) relied on collective open forums that rewarded success and offered smaller incentives for lesser contributions, such as product feedback.

There were no rules or restrictions on innovation. Individuals were responsible for the objects they made and released into the world. Cyber-Smith City, saturated in nanotechnological applications, grew atom-by-atom with 3D printers to specify tolerances that included bicycles, cars, small airplanes, weapons, and solar panels.

Open-source innovation was not without societal inequities when an epidemic of refugees combined with human traffic solicitation. Although a degree of social entrepreneurship innovation was offered to the public, Stan Smith began placing more emphasis on closed collaboration innovation, which pushed more power within an elite decision-making body, which in the case of Cyber-Smith City was held by an elite government-industry partnership. The public became subjected to its decisions.

As innovative collaboration switched priorities from public to elite forces, large-scale investments poured resources into areas such as national defense systems and high-end cybernetics. The closed collaboration innovation concept also shifted focus on integrating nanotechnology into large systems for increasing system control in the security arena.

Programmable machines that printed 3D structures and functional objects made nanotechnology ubiquitous for the elite class. This perpetuated negative externalities, including the continued segregation of socioeconomic classes and centralized control.

TWENTY-FOUR – The Evil Enterprise

By 2022, Smith Robotics, Inc., became the leader in creating the most human-like robots. These so-called humanoids were developed with a full range of human facial expressions and functional body parts. Stan's goal, at least his explicitly stated goal, was to develop the most engaging human-like robots that could establish a deep, trusted relationship with people.

Smith's current project combined a joint venture with MarsX, which planned a mission to Mars by 2025. Surrounded by a superb team of roboticists, AI experts, scientists, technologists, hardware/software engineers, and cognitive specialists, Smith and his counterpart Edwin Mann built a spacecraft with the aid of former NASA engineers. While Smith's team developed androids, so sophisticated, it was close to impossible to distinguish them from humans with the naked eye, Manns team completed a Mars Colonial Transporter and spacesuits developed for extensive life support on Mars.

Smith's idea focused on the humanoid's function on Mars without life support suits because the life sustaining aspects of survival planned an integrated circuit within their creative structure.

Both men developed a two-stage plan that would send a spacecraft to Mars consisting of these humanoids as a test. Their plan relied on generating rocket propellant by reacting hydrogen into the atmosphere on Mars. Once on the planet, the humanoids would build a fabricated living space for human habitation and the beginnings of a Martian City.

Every team member from both fields swore to loyalty. They were dedicated to building human-like machines that could function in every capacity as a human, their mental state, emotional, physical, and social. These droids would be able to study in school, work at jobs, fall in love, and raise families. It was their mission to infuse artificial intelligence with the whole gambit of human intelligence and emotions by interaction in every way, even beyond dialog.

The planned flight to Mars at the end of the year would consist of the latest humanoid version emerging from Smith Robotics, Inc. Mann, and his team of engineers, all of whom designed the spacecraft to take advantage of the space photons emitting radiation, planned the trip to Mars.

They would leverage this scientific occurrence by incorporating a thin carbon fiber sail that propels the ship's launch to the front of Mars on its orbital path. As a result, the planet would catch the craft in its gravitational pull.

Smith's robots were unique in that they were created with the ability to simulate unparalleled interactive, human-like facial features with the integration of leading-edge innovations in materials, hardware, software, aesthetics, characters, and stories. Some of these features included the emulation of over seventy facial and neck muscular architectures, machine vision via micro-cameras inside the eyes, lightweight portability, and self-efficient microchip operational functionality.

ய

Doctor Gray led a small tour of scientists, engineers, students, media, and defense industry representatives.

"Our robots exhibit the highest quality expressions and interactivity in the world, fusing our advances in walking, talking robots who maintain eye contact, recognize faces, and understand speech, hold conversations, and simulate a real person's personality. All of this is achieved through our advanced Artificial Intelligence, called the Character Engine."

"Dr. Gray, if I may?"

"Yes, and you are with…?"

"The Smithsonian."

"Yes, please. What is your question?"

"You have talked about the benefits of your latest models towards human support in medicine, education, and other benefactors, but what about the risk of their combat capabilities?"

"What about them? The armies of the world could use them to maintain a peaceful world order. If there were any rebellious outbreaks in the hotspots of the world, they could be dispatched to resolve the situation permanently, without any more of our children going off and dying in wars created by politicians sitting behind fancy desks."

"But wouldn't you be afraid of these—these androids turning on us, that is, not being able to distinguish between the so-called 'good guys and bad guys?'"

There was murmuring within the crowd. "No, no, no. We program them in such a way that this would make it impossible."

"But…"

"In fact, I'll tell you what. Why don't I take you to a demonstration we have scheduled to show just how well these particular models perform in a hostage taking situation?"

"Yes, I would like to see such a demonstration," another voice yelled.

"Very well, Miss…"

"Assaf," Lyna said, holding out her hand. "Dr. Abigail Assaf, of Tshai Institute."

"Ah, yes, Dr. Assaf! My apologies. I was not aware that you were part of this group today. I did not even bother to check the guest list. I would very much like to show you a demonstration."

"Thank you, Dr. Gray."

"Shall we make it a date for tomorrow afternoon, say 2:00 PM?"

"2:00 PM, it is!"

"Wonderful!" Dr. Gray continued leading the tour, taking the small crowd to individual models. "Now this one, we call Julie. With her, we have integrated natural language processing with ASR, TTS, computer vision, artistry, and narrative so that you can have a natural, interactive conversation with Julie. Go ahead, ask her something."

Someone from the crowd raised his voice. "How are you doing, Julie?"

The human-looking blonde girl scanned the crowd until her eyes focused on the man who asked the question. "Everything is going very well, thank you."

The man beamed with a smile as those around him clapped their pleasure.

"Now, then," Dr. Gray continued. "We have software that allows Julie the advanced capacity for interaction with people. This software combines the work of writers who author the robot's dialogue using 'chabot' tools, with natural language to simulate a human conversation. Julie also uses computer vision, including face tracking and face recognition, to simulate complete verbal and nonverbal interaction, such as maintaining eye contact and turning to follow fellow conversationalists."

As the crowd moved to the next model on display, another man walked closer to Julie and said, "You are quite attractive."

Julie looked at the man and answered with a wink and a smile, "Why, thank you. I am made to love."

Dr. Gray's raised voice startled the man. "Now over here, we have another humanoid robot which can mimic human expressions and hold simple interactive conversations with the crowd. This one responds with a touch of a button using a mobile phone app. His name is Wolf. He can smile, wince, frown, wink, or even act drunk."

The crowd chuckled.

"Wolf can also respond to his environment, thanks to several cameras inside his eyes and chest. Go ahead and ask him something."

A female voice from the crowd called out, "Are you trained in combat?"

There was more murmuring in the crowd. "It's all right, folks. Go ahead and answer the lady, Wolf."

"I am trained in combat and in love. For which would you like me to demonstrate?"

As the crowd's reaction was mixed with laughter and surprise, Dr. Gray added, "Neither one today, Wolf, but thank you."

"Any time, Dr. Gray."

"Let's move on to the next one. Here we have Dina, another humanoid robot consisting of memories, feelings, and beliefs. She engages in conversation with other humans, such as offering an emotional account of her brother's personality changes after returning home from the Iraq War. Dina, go ahead and tell these folks a little about your brother who was an Iraqi Freedom vet."

"Okay, well, he was never the same person. He once was so full of life and vigor, but after returning from two tours to Iraq, he stopped smiling. He was no longer interested in doing the things he had in the past."

The people in the crowd talked among themselves. An older man said, "I was in Iraq during that time. What unit was he with?"

"He was with the 82nd Airborne and served time in Fallujah."

"That's who I was with and where I served. What was his name?"

"His name was Michael Snider, and he was a sergeant."

"MY GOD!" the man exclaimed. "I know him, and—and you're right! He was never the same after…"

"Why don't we move along to the rest of the tour, and maybe we can talk about war stories later, huh?"

Those in the crowd agreed. "Yes, good idea," someone volunteered.

Turning to his wife, the man said, "This is unbelievable. Mikey did have a younger sister named Dina."

As Dr. Gray continued with the group, Abigail was busy taking mental notes, adding some of the technological details she was not familiar with before the tour. Now, she continued to add some of the technological features that enabled these functional androids to perform.

There was one that was battery-powered with an untethered walking body and full human-like expressions. The fascinating part was the fact that he functioned with life-like expressions and full mobility for hours on AA batteries.

Then there was the one that was a baby, equipped with high-definition cameras in the eyes and programmed to interact as a baby would do with his or her mother. The tour group could not carry cameras, so Abigail retained these images in her photographic memory.

Dr. Gray murmured in the background of her consciousness, "We developed machine-learning methods to analyze face-to-face interaction between mothers and infants, to extract the social controller used by infants, and to port it to this baby we call Baby Doe. Note the baby's expressions. They are important to establish a relationship and communicate intuitively with people."

"Sir, if I may?" a reporter began.

"Yes, what is it?"

"Can you explain to the public what the difference is between an android and a cyborg?"

Dr. Gray seemed insulted by the question. "Sure. An android is a robot made to look and act like a human being, with experts in the field giving them emotions. On the other hand, a cyborg is a living organism that has robotic or mechanical parts meant to extend their capabilities. In most cases, the robotic parts are integrated into the organism and cannot be removed."

"Furthermore," Dr. Gray continued, "people who have mechanical and electrical implants like pacemakers and robotic limbs can already be called cyborgs, for example, since the non-organic parts are meant to extend their capabilities. You see, androids are human in form but cannot be considered living beings, or at least not legally anyway. An android that dies can be repaired and reactivated just like any machine, but if a cyborg dies, there is no way that the organic part can be repaired."

"So, bottom line is that an android is a robot that resembles a human being, while a cyborg is an organism that is part organic and part machine?"

"Yes, you could put it that way, I suppose. We are experimenting with a new concept involving mind transfer, which is the idea of transferring consciousness from one who has paid to have his consciousness transferred into a new body."

There was more chatter from the crowd. "Wouldn't that affect the person whose consciousness is being transferred?"

"Theoretically, yes; however, in the past, our work consisted of donors who were either terminally ill or had already died. Now, since we have found no side effects from the transferor, we have begun with volunteers who are healthy."

"Volunteers?"

"Yes, of course! Volunteers!" Dr. Gray answered with an agitated voice as if insulted by the insinuation. Before he could direct the crowd to the last subject, there was another question.

"Can you tell us how this process works? I am very intrigued."

"Well, Miss…?"

"Jordan. Hannah Jordan," Lyna volunteered. "She is with me, my protégé. I also call her *The Millennial Girl*."

"I see," Dr. Assaf said. "Well, as I mentioned before…"

"Please address her, Dr. Gray. She is very capable of deriving her own questions and responses."

"Of course." Dr. Gray walked up to examine Asha. "Remarkable—truly remarkable. To answer your question, Miss Jordan, we tried various measures, but the most successful to date was with the transfer of a spinal cord that included the full spectrum of the brain."

"Wouldn't the brain still need to be alive or active for the transfer to be successful?" Asha asked.

Dr. Gray glanced at Lyna, who quipped, "Her specialty is in the medical department."

Looking back at Asha, he responded, "Not when we are equipped with all the transferring processes necessary to ensure success. As you may know, when there is no blood pumped to the brain, the nerve cells in the cerebral cortex die in two minutes. So of course, we use stored blood transfusions. The nerve cells in the midbrain that control unconscious activity such as breathing can last thirty minutes, and the nerve cells in the spinal cord can last an hour without blood flow."

"But how would the brain store the oxygen? The nerve cells require oxygen and glucose to function. If the heart were not pumping, the oxygen in the stagnant blood would be used up by the cerebral cortex in two minutes."

"Yes, indeed. You do know your human anatomy. Keep in mind, our transfers are designed for an android fit. However, to answer your question, the cerebral cortex must be capable of receiving input, such as sound for example, interpreted by the auditory cortex. Our conceivable notion focused on the midbrain, where there might be some emotional recognition, which was our primary goal."

"Kind of like the surgical procedure accomplished twenty-four years ago on the twin babies who were conjoined at the head?"

"Precisely, Miss Jordan. You know your history as well. Did Dr. Assaf have you attend Harvard or Yale?"

There was some laughter from the crowd.

"I was accepted there, as well as The Military Academy at West Point," Asha answered with pride. "However, I did not attend either one." She regrated revealing anything personal about herself, especially after the humor seemed to disappear from Dr. Gray's face. There was a hushed silence.

"Then you may not be aware that the two girls shared a cranial cavity."

"Yes, I am. Their brains were partially fused."

"Indeed, they were. Their brains enmeshed more than expected, so it took the surgeons, operating in shifts, more than four days. In fact, the surgeons had to individually coagulate, separate, and divide the blood vessels between the two brains."

There were gasps within the crowd. Watching Asha for a response, he added, "The brains were wrapped around each other like a helix. Quite a remarkable operation, I must say."

"Yes, it was," Asha agreed. "We studied this case and found it amazing that the skull was refashioned with some bone material and Gore-Tex fibers. The surgeons used 3D scans with computer-imaging technology."

"Very impressive, Miss Jordan. Ladies and gentlemen, the reason I allowed this conversation to go on in earshot of you all is because it was this very procedure and the technology used in it that inspired Mr. Stan Smith with this type of cyber engineering with humanoids. The best part about the whole operation was its success. Both girls lived until the age of seven. Although one died, the other is now twenty-three."

The crowd cheered.

"Should I ask you what your major was, Miss Jordan?"

"I studied pre-medical courses—Advanced Medical Technologies in cybernetics was my specialty. I was involved with cytogenetic research, which covered the integration of cyborg and human-space technology."

"Why am I not surprised?" Dr. Gray began to walk on. "Finally, ladies and gentlemen, this last model will bring us to the end of our tour. Jan Chapman is an android, although there is no way you could tell it, and she is being programmed for a different kind of mission, one I am not able to discuss now. However, I do want you to see this demonstration."

As the crowd inched closer to Jan, Asha tried not to let on because she was aware that Abigail had been studying her ever since she volunteered her knowledge. Another visitor, a male executive from India, joked with the robot, "I think you would make a perfect wife for me."

Looking at him with an annoyed facial expression, she replied, "I seriously doubt it. You're not my type."

The crowd erupted in laughter while the executive slithered away. Then to everyone's astonishment, Jan continued.

"No offense, but I have my own free will."

Dr. Gray interrupted, "Jan is made with an elastic polymer, a special substance used with our latest models for the human-like robot heads that can serve a range of functions, where face-to-face communications are important. Well, the time is up, and I'm afraid this will end the tour for today."

Everybody in the crowd cheered as a couple of assistants led them towards the exit. "Oh, Dr. Assaf, I wanted to get back with you about tomorrow's demonstration. I was wondering if you wouldn't mind bringing along your protégé, Miss Jordan, that is, if you do not mind," he added, looking right at Asha.

Lyna and Asha exchanged glances. "She is more than welcome to come along. Hannah?"

"I would love to join you!"

TWENTY-FIVE - Trauma

The abrupt opening of the door startled Nicole from her bed. She watched as a man in a business suit entered the room.

"Nicole? Nicole Anderson?"

"Yes," she whispered. "That is my name. Who are you?"

The man flipped on the light and walked towards her. "You don't recognize me?"

Nicole studied his features. "No, I am sorry, but I do not know who you are."

Taking a couple steps closer, he continued. "I am sorry you do not remember me, but you, along with many other promising young interns, came to my office for a seminar and social gathering."

"I—I remember the…wait! You—you are the man that oversaw…"

"The Office of Intelligence and Analysis. Yes, I am the Under Secretary, David Cranston."

"I do remember you now! Will you take me home, Mr. Cranston?" Nicole asked, hope in her voice.

David chuckled. "Of course, I will, Nicole. That's why I came." Before he could finish what, he was about to say next, Nicole jumped from her bed, elated, and wrapped her arms around him.

"Oh, thank God you came! I just knew somebody would find me and take me home, and Makeala, too, right?"

David was not smiling when he answered, "Yes, of course. I came to get both of you and take you back home."

"Oh, thank God!" she exclaimed. David Cranston returned her hug of gratitude firmly, holding her up against him without any sign of releasing her. Nicole's expression changed as she tried to remove herself from his firm grip. "Mr. Cranston, you can let me go now, please."

David continued to hold her against him. "I will, Nicole…soon." As his hands moved across her back, she struggled more vigorously to be free from his hold, but David pushed her onto the bed and moved to clamp her down.

Nicole screamed and kicked, but he was too powerful. "STOP! PLEASE STOP!"

"It will be okay."
"NOOO! WHY?"

The door sprung open, and the lights came on, causing Cranston to jump up in a fury. "I was supposed to be undisturbed for one hour!" he shouted.

Stella answered, "Mr. Smith requests your presence at once!"

"You ignorant robotic droid. Can't you see…?"

"He said it was urgent."

Nicole jumped off the bed and cowered on the floor in the corner of the room, shaking.

The large man behind Stella came in to lead Cranston out the door as Stella followed behind him. She glanced at Nicole, who was still huddled in the corner, crying. Then she turned off the light and locked the door.

The big man, Tanner, who was with Stella, led Cranston into the surveillance room, where Stan Smith was sitting in front of a big screen 3D television. A security agent was at the controls. Samantha, his personal assistant, three bodyguards, the Head of Security, and Dr. Gray flanked him. "Sorry for the interruption, Mr. Secretary, but I couldn't wait. Do you know her?"

David Cranston, looking agitated, walked over to the screen to see who they were watching. Angry by the manner of summons, he snapped, "No. Should I?"

Smith detected his tension and answered, "Look again! This time focus on something other than your personal appetites for the young and innocent," he replied tersely.

Insulted by the remark, Cranston studied the screen more closely. "Wait—wait a minute! That's the female Green Beret...um—Sergeant Hawkins!"

"Yes, we know who she is. Her DNA is all over her room. My question is whether or not you know her?"

"Not personally, no. I attended a ceremony once where she was being honored, and we exchanged a ceremonial handshake."

"So why is she here, Mr. Secretary? You have something planned we don't know about?"

Cranston nervously answered, "No—no, of course not! Why would I try anything that stupid and implicate myself in the process?"

"Indeed, I wondered the same thing."

"You can't possibly think…"

"No, I do not think you are involved. However, something is going down, and I am going to find out what it is, Mr. Secretary. And for your sake, I would make a massive attempt to contact our clients and find out what she is up to, wouldn't you agree?"

"I agree, Mr. Smith, and will get right on it."

"You might want to pay a personal visit to your friend as well, to find out what she knows."

"Nicole wouldn't…"

"I was not referring to her, Mr. Secretary. You do have another interest, I believe, the one with the purple hair."

"You mean Jericha. Yes. I will visit her after my phone calls."

"Good. Dr. Gray will join you for the questioning."

"Of course."

"She is attractive, you know. She would make an excellent replica, don't you think?"

"Yes—yes, she would. I'll see to it."

Cranston was ushered out of the room by the same bodyguard who brought him in.

Smith looked at Dr. Gray. "I want to know everything about this Dr. Abigail's role with this Green Beret girl."

"So, Hannah Jordan is Sergeant Asha Hawkins," Dr. Gray replied. "Wow! She was quite impressive during the tour if I say so myself."

"Samantha." The tall, eloquent, brown-haired woman came to his side. "Get a background check on Sergeant Asha Hawkins. I want to know everything about her."

"You got it."

Looking back at Dr. Gray, Smith said, "I have an idea for our soldier girl."

"Oh?"

"Cyrix! She's programmed to stop short of a kill if she detects her opponent as being human. You can fix all of that, can't you, Dr. Gray?"

"Yes, of course. Since I am the medical examiner for all the droids, including Cyrix, I will simply make any changes during her pre-fight exam. And if Dr. Roberts questions me?"

"Just tell him that you have other urgent matters to address and will not have the opportunity to check later. First, I want you to join the secretary, Cranston, and see how much you can persuade that brazen girl with the nose ring to tell you all she knows."

"I'll be able to convince her, I'm sure."

"You always do. Once you get what we need, have your team take her to area seventy-one to prepare her for replication."

"What about Cranston?"

"Make sure he stays with you. He, along with our many other guests, will join us for a special pre-fight luncheon tomorrow at noon."

"You are going into Phase III now?"

"I believe we have to move everything up in light of the situation, don't you, Dr. Gray?"

"I'll get on it straight away."

"Take care of the girl first, and then do whatever you need to do to make sure Cyrix is ready for Friday night. Then, be sure to invite Sergeant Hawkins and whoever Dr. Assaf is for lunch."

"Our identity scan was unable to trace who she is?"

"It claimed she is Lyna Al-Jamil, of the CIA."

"Well…"

"…and Chloé Dubois, of the French intelligence…and whoever else she might be."

"My God!"

"Bring them both to the master's chambers tomorrow at noon. I have an offer that neither will be able to refuse."

Smith's intelligence forces, led by Dr. Ernest Gray, were able to discover in detail the plan launched by the President of the United States to topple his empire.

"This one was very clever, one of the best we've seen," Dr. Gray reported to Smith. "Had she succeeded with her attempt to penetrate our centralized system, they, or whoever we're dealing with here, could have destroyed your operation!"

This revelation caused Smith much anguish. "How could she have accomplished this? Is she a humanoid?"

"No, she is very human. We had to discover the truth the hard way."

"Tell me you didn't kill her!"

"Oh no, no, no. You just don't kill somebody with that intelligence."

"You're right!" Smith jumped up and touched the screen on his desk, giving him a live feed of the replication room. "Cease operations on this one, at once!"

The head of MarsX transformation, Doctor Thomas Whittleton, walked to the screen. "Is that you, Mr. Smith?"

"Yes, it is! The purple-haired girl, Jericha. Tell me I'm not too late!"

"For transformation?"

"Yes."

"You are just in time."

"Cease operations at once! Keep her in holding until further notice. Be sure to give her the best medical treatment."

"Will do, sir."

"Thank you, Dr. Whittleton."

380 | SCOTT MEEHAN

Looking at Dr. Gray, Smith continued. "What else did you find out?"

"Well, the main thing is that our soldier girl is the brains behind the operation."

"Sergeant Hawkins?"

"Yes…and there is a third."

"Doctor Abigail Assaf?"

"Now, that is what's troubling. Everything she told us about the third girl does not match up with this Dr. Assaf."

"Maybe she was trained in deceptive descriptions."

"We interrogated her for that possibility, but our expert believes that there is still another girl besides Dr. Assaf."

"Great, so we have this Abigail, whoever she is, and another girl on the loose somewhere."

"So, it would seem."

"We have no time to waste. Contact those two and let them know that the tour will begin two hours earlier than planned. Then bring them straight to my master's chambers. I will have a nice lunch prepared for them. Cyrix is ready?"

"Yes! Took care of everything myself. What do you have in mind?"

"When you arrive with the two of them, you will introduce them to me. I, in turn, will introduce them to all our guests, including Cyrix. In time, I will make a proposal to Dr. Assaf that she won't be able to refuse."

"Oh?"

"Her protégé, Hannah Jordan, will fight Cyrix Friday night in front of millions."

A wry grin creased Dr. Gray's leathery face. "The human will not stand a chance."

"Precisely, but Cyrix will give everybody a good show first."

"Wait a minute. If the human is destroyed in front of millions, the world will see that you crossed the line by matching your droid with a human."

"Not if she goes waterborne."

"Waterborne?"

Smith stood up from his desk with a conniving smile. "Yes, for the first time in history, our UAFC ring will be without ropes and in the middle of an Olympic-sized pool."

Dr. Gray began to laugh. "You are a genius!"

"So I am, so I am. This way, nobody will be able to tell that she was a human. No blood and guts because Cyrix will drown her, and everybody will think that this Millennial Girl had malfunctioned by being under the water for too long."

"The Americans and whoever else is collaborating with them in this will come down on you like…"

"That is why I will initiate Contingency IV."

"But the ship may not be ready! It isn't scheduled to be completed for another three months!"

"That's what I had the media believe. However, it is quite ready, Dr. Gray."

"Alright! I am on my way."

TWENTY-SIX – The Fight

Stan Smith took the mixed martial arts challenge, known for years as the "Ultimate Fighting Championship," to new levels when he introduced android fighting in 2121. Inside his spacious juxtaposition, vintage-futuristic coliseum, the fights televised worldwide on Friday nights. There was always a capacity crowd, and viewers from around the world had turned the event into the number-one rated international sporting episode, surpassing soccer, cricket, and racing.

Smith's specialty featured his own champion, the female droid known to the world as Cyrix. Specially designed in every humanoid facet, one of her specialties was her hand-to-hand combat skills. Four years before the fights became popular, Smith had solicited the best humanoid engineers around the world who specialized in defense systems. Dr. Roberts, an American cybernetic engineer, demonstrated Cyrix, who proved to be a superior humanoid over the rest. Nobody thought it strange that Dr. Roberts modeled her after his deceased wife and treated her as his own possession. When Dr. Roberts won the multi-million-dollar contract with Smith Robotics, Inc., he continued to hone her combat arts skills during maintenance and upgrades.

It took Smith a lot of convincing of Roberts to have him agree to the fighting competition. During another global demonstration, this one on hand-to-hand fighting, Cyrix once again proved to be the most superior model ever witnessed. Over a period of two years, Cyrix became the world champion, having never lost a fight. Thanks to Dr. Roberts, she was not just the best humanoid fighter, but she was also incredibly beautiful.

There had been no model coming close to defeating Cyrix in the UAFC, and many speculated that she used a fraction of her capabilities during the fights to prolong the match. She was the model future soldier and a prototype study for many national defenses.

In the master's chambers, a large banquet table was covered in a silk white tablecloth. The room was full of VIPs, and there were two leather-backed, empty chairs at the head of the table where Smith sat. When the solid brass doors opened, Asha and Lyna exchanged uneasy glances when they saw the many guests of honor staring at them. These were dignitaries, government agents and department heads. "Welcome, ladies!" Smith bellowed as he stood. "Please join us."

Dr. Gray motioned them towards the head of the table. "Right this way, please."

Asha noticed two large men blocking the door that they just came through. Both women walked towards the front. Stan Smith came around and began his introduction. "Everybody, these are the two I have been telling you about, Dr. Abigail Assaf and her protégé, Hannah Jordan. You would never be able to tell, but Hannah is a humanoid, just like our Cyrix here."

The dignitaries studied the two women. Asha saw that many were leaning over to the person next to them and whispering something. Two dozen luminaries sat around the table, but her eyes focused on the one she recognized as the Secretary of the Army, who was speaking to the Secretary of the Navy. Not too many people knew she could read lips.

"Yep, that's her, Sergeant Asha Hawkins."

"Allow me to introduce you to all of our guests," Smith continued before introducing them to everyone in the room. Asha kept her focus on the American heads of state, including the Secretary of the Army, the Secretary of the Navy, Director of Biometric Identity Management, the Under Secretary for the Office of Intelligence and Analysis, and the Director of Homeland Security. The presence of this many high-ranking American officials disturbed her.

Lyna's interest focused more on the French and Arab delegates and one other man. The one who stared at her with the blazing blue eyes and strands of blond hair mixed with white. He managed a quick smirk when Lyna looked at him.

After the formalities, Smith said, "Please. Sit down. I am tired now." That remark brought about some laughter.

"Join us in a special meal together, and then, Dr. Assaf, I wish to make a toast and a proposal to you that will be so—so exhilarating!"

Lyna looked surprised before exchanging glances with Asha. "Thank you very much, Mr. Smith. It is an honor."

"The pleasure is mine, trust me."

During the meal, the talk centered on the state of the world in relation to cybernetics, flights to Mars, the current water drought in much of the world, and the latest in defense systems. Some questions geared towards Asha's attributes beyond her intellect.

"So, Dr. Assaf, I was told about how advanced your Hannah is. Tell me, is she also trained in the basic combat arts?"

"Yes, she is, in fact."

"Splendid, splendid!" Looking at Lyna, Stan continued. "So, Dr. Assaf, here is my proposal. It is quite simple. I would like very much for your young protégé to fight Cyrix in the ring tomorrow night."

There was some murmuring around the table before Lyna answered, "Mr. Smith, I—I don't know what to say."

"Well, say you will accept the challenge, of course! Matching two humanoids with such intellect will attract world attention!"

Before Lyna could respond, Asha looked at Cyrix and said, "I will gladly fight your champion, Cyrix, Mr. Smith."

"What? Hannah!" Lyna began.

"Excellent, Hannah! Excellent!" Smith yelled as he stood up with a glass in his hand. Those around the table followed suit. "Here's to the most exciting fight ever! In fact, henceforth, we will call this fight, *The world champion, Cyrix, versus The Millennial Girl!*"

In shock, Lyna looked at Asha, who was straining to hide her emotions by keeping her gaze fixed on Cyrix.

Stan Smith looked at Cyrix, who was also staring at Asha. A broad smile crossed his face.

ᛟ

Seven hours before the fight, Asha was feeling more nervous than she could ever remember. Although her confidence level in her own ability was high, this would be a first against a humanoid defense system. With the match set for this very night, one that would broadcast to several hundred million homes, including the stadiums own 3-D satellite big screen, Asha strolled out the door.

"Where are you going?" Lyna asked.

"To the lounge...to think."

"I'll come with you."

"No, please. I need some time alone."

Lyna looked puzzled. "Okay. You know where to find me if you need me."

Asha forced a grin. "Yes."

Lyna let her go but uttered a stern warning, "You know this is a trap."

Asha looked back at Lyna but did not respond before continuing to the lounge.

The humanoid bartender, Nick, walked up to Asha, who was sitting alone. "You are the Millennial Girl."

Asha watched him for a second and decided to play along before answering. "Yes."

"A pleasure to meet you."

"You are...?"

393 | SCOTT MEEHAN

"Nick. Just Nick. I will let you in on a little secret. I am like you."

"Like me?"

"Yes, you know." Nick leaned closer to Ashas face and whispered, "A droid."

Asha smiled. "Really? I would not have guessed."

"Thank you for saying so. What can I get you? Anything at all. It's on the house."

"That's kind of you. How about just a Merlot?"

"Sure thing, but won't that affect your circuits?"

Asha laughed. "No, I am the latest AMX designed anthropomorphic android, featuring more than 100 human characteristic algorithms," she joked.

"Wow! What company is doing this? I mean, what is your lifespan?"

"Not so much a company as it is a government, but I am not allowed to know what country. As for lifespan, I am told after 40 years I can be recharged with upgrades and live an additional 40 years."

Nick stared at her, studying her movements. "They made you special. I cannot tell at all that you are an android."

"I'll take that as a compliment."

"Are you ready to face our own champion, Cyrix?"

"Yes. I believe so."

"She has a lot of the same features you have, except her eyes do not focus as well as yours do."

"She is beautiful and strong."

"As for strength, you will find out tonight. And her beauty, you be the judge, here she comes now."

Asha turned to see Cyrix approaching her. Taking a seat next to Asha, she said, "I'll have the usual, Nick."

"Here you are! Already made."

Asha noticed her sipping a bluish-green liquid from a spiral glass. When Cyrix turned to face her, she just smiled.

"So, we meet again."

Nick looked surprised. "You two have met already?"

Asha took a sip of her wine and set the glass down. "Yes."

Nick looked at Cyrix. "The Millennial Girl said she was designed to live for 50 years and could be upgraded for another 50 years!"

Cyrix put her drink down and looked at Asha. "Who, besides a government, can design a humanoid with such longevity?"

"Dr. Abigail Assaf, of Tshai Institute," Asha answered.

"Hmm, so she tells you."

Asha did not make eye contact with her but stared at the spiral glass. "Yes. I believe her."

Cyrix turned to face Asha. "Could you join me outside on the patio for a moment, please?"

"I am not sure that would be such a good idea."

Cyrix's eyes turned different shades of yellow and green before she was able to look straight into Ashas eyes. "Please?"

Something about her facial expression and her changed voice caught Ashas attention. "Okay, sure."

"Thank you." Looking at Nick, she said, "Please excuse us."

Nick did not answer but watched as both women walked out the glass enclosure onto the patio. Once outside, Cyrix looked at Asha, trying to focus, her eyes changing colors. "You are a human being, aren't you?"

Asha was not sure how to answer, not knowing whether Cyrix knew of Smith's plot. "What did Mr. Smith tell you?"

"That you were a sophisticated droid and that I should destroy you in the water because your design weakness would be there."

"Water?"

"Yes, he plans to move the floors surrounding the ring, which will reveal a large pool. His major surprise to the world. I am to take you in the water and hold you under. This way, he could prove that I, his design, was superior. He does not believe that you could endure the water."

Asha started to ask more questions, but Dr. Roberts approached them. "Is everything alright, dear?"

"Yes, I was just getting acquainted with my opponent."

"And I was just returning to my quarters," Asha answered.

"Ah, Hannah. Before you leave, could you please remain a moment while I speak with Cyrix off the record?"

Asha looked at him and hesitated.

"Please, just one minute longer."

"Okay, I will wait." Asha watched the two of them conversing, Dr. Roberts with his back towards Asha. If Cyrix was communicating, she did not use her lips. Both approached her.

"Thank you for waiting, Hannah."

"Everything okay, Dr. Roberts?"

"Yes, my apologies. I will not hold you any longer."

Before she walked away, Cyrix left her some departing words. "Have you ever heard of the *kiss of death*?"

Asha turned to face her. "Isn't that the last thing you do to your opponent before you destroy them?"

Cyrix smiled. "Yes, so you have seen it."

"Once or twice."

"Good! You must be prepared for the *kiss of death* tonight. Your life will depend on it."

Asha looked at her before departing.

"Cyrix? Are you okay?" Dr. Roberts asked.

"This new permanence algorithm. Is it real?"

"I'm not sure."

Cyrix tried to focus on Roberts, her eyes moving and changing colors. "I want to live."

"Then you know what you must do tonight."

Cyrix nodded her head in agreement. "There is something you should know," Cyrix added.

"What is it?"

"Dr. Gray."

"What about him?"

"He does not think that I can see or think when he places me in hibernation state for medical evaluation…but I can see and feel everything."

"WHAT—what are you saying? What are you telling me, Cyrix?"

Her eyes moved in a flash, with the color changing with increased frequency. Looking at him, eyes out of focus, she added mechanically, "I am sorry! I did not know. He said he would destroy me if I ever told anyone."

"Enough!" Holding her, he added, "I will take care of Dr. Gray myself. You—you must complete this mission tonight."

TWENTY-SEVEN – Losing Battle

Asha looked perplexed standing next to Lyna at the tunnel entrance. She helped train Asha the best she could in the time they had. "I watched her perform during a demonstration. She was like a speeding missile underwater! The technology behind her is something we have never seen before in our labs. It was astounding!"

She looked at Lyna but remained silent. Confident in her own martial arts ability, Asha mastered karate, jiu-jitsu, muay thai, tae kwon do, boxing, kickboxing, wrestling, and judo. It was because of these skills that the Mossad had sought her services for this mission, believing Asha was their chance of getting inside the Smith industrial network.

Although android contestants can tap the floor or verbally notify the referee that they do not wish to continue, Cyrix had never experienced the tap. Since she was the undefeated champion fighting android, there was little doubt that Asha would have to destroy Cyrix. It was her only option of survival.

Asha rehearsed the various forms of technique involving striking and grappling. She focused on striking blows with hands, feet, knees, or elbows. With Lyna, they practiced the grappling techniques of submissions, chokeholds, throws and takedowns.

What Asha knew that even Lyna did not know, was the fact that during her surgery, she had bionic implants of her own. She would use these attributes to her favor.

Stan Smith enacted many of the rules himself, based on the existing ones from the UFC regulations that had been in existence since 2001. Some were the basics, such as the duration of the round length, having a ringside referee, and fighting in a standard fighting area. Unique to android fighting was using android class-level specifications with models designed after a certain year.

Other examples included the fighting area with the padded canvas measures eighteen feet by eighteen feet and thirty-two feet by thirty-two feet, and four feet above the floor of the building, containing suitable steps or a ramp for use by the participants. There was no metal fence enclosed around the fighting area to prevent a fall out or break through onto the floor or spectators.

Each contestant chose his or her own uniform, another difference between the UFC and UAFC. However, everyone was required to walk through a scanner prior to entering the ring.

The match was scheduled for five rounds of five-minute durations.

"Last-minute advice?"

Lyna smirked. "Focus. Remember your training. This is combat now!"

"Do I stand a chance?"

"God only knows, but you have a relationship with him, right? Ask, and you shall receive."

"She has great kickboxing techniques and uses them to ground her opponents," Asha inserted.

"But you know how to defend against that. Concentrate."

"She also has a lot of power, as demonstrated with some knockout right hooks."

"You know how to defend against that also. You, my dear Asha, understand strategy, and you possess lightning speed."

"My normal strategies may be of no use against an android."

"Okay, tell me what's bothering you. This isn't like you."

Asha took a deep breath. "Cyrix knows I'm human."

"WHAT? How?"

"I don't know, but she approached me at the bar late last night."

"What did she say? How did she know?"

"She figured it out during our conversation, I think. Her circuits were sending conflicting signals, or at least that is what she said."

"I wish you would have come to me."

407 | SCOTT MEEHAN

"I—I did not want you to pull me out of the fight. She also told me about the water…beneath the floor."

"What?"

"And she warned me to be prepared for the *Kiss of Death*, that my life depended on it."

Lyna reacted as if someone struck her across the face. Then she put her hand on her arm. "Be strong, like your father."

Ashas eyes narrowed, looking at Lyna. "What?"

"He confronted death…evil, square in the eye, and came out a victor."

"How—how…"

"A miracle. It was a miracle! I never believed in them until then."

"How will I stand a chance with her if I am forced in the water?"

"You will do okay. Use your skills and techniques, or else…"

"Or else no more Asha."

Lyna looked back at her with deep concern. "You can do this. Pray."

"I do. I pray hard all the time."

"You do that because you'll need divine intervention for this. If she defeats you, Smith's program will move forward unimpeded, and the whole human race could suffer the consequences."

"You have quite a way of putting that into perspective."

"How about this one? Which creator will be victorious this evening, hum?"

Before she could answer, the intercom blared the song *Mutuality,* by Orka Veera, and then rocketed into the beat of psychedelic-techno music to the delight of the crowds. A vast array of lights splashed across the coliseum, followed by a blend of solid colors and shades of hybrid designs day and night sky, flowers, orchids, oceans. Laser technology dazzled the audience with an array of colorful displays.

Stan Smith himself walked to the center of the ring. "Ladies, gentlemen, and global droids. On behalf of Smith Robotics, Inc., and CyberSmith City, allow me to welcome you to the Ultimate Android Fighting Challenge!"

The throng roared their pleasure to the Smith's standard opening at center ring, Samantha Stone at his side. The spotlight widened to reveal the whole fighting ring, which was for the first time without ropes.

Smith continued, "And further, a surprise for your entertaining pleasure, both fighters will prove that with the latest design technology, they can fight and survive just as well in the water."

The spotlight widened further, exposing the ring standing alone, surrounded by a body of water from a one hundred meter in diameter swimming pool. The crowd's reaction was mixed with wonder and applause. Three walkways extended from the ring, one connected to the VIP area, where Stan Smith led Samantha to an already seated group of VIPs, and the other two from the fighter's entrance.

"And now, I take immense pleasure in introducing our latest challenger…created by Dr. Abigail Assaf, of Tshai Institute…*The Millennial Girl!*

There was an admirable amount of cheering for Asha as she walked towards the center ring wearing a one-piece, black latex, carbon fiber ensemble. Her outfit was a type-A, luminance distortion model, one of the benefits of being answerable to the president. Her gaze avoided the audience as she stared straight ahead towards her opponent.

"Aaaaand, our very own world champion! *Cyrix*!" The crowd roared its approval with the music changing to *We are the Champions,* by Queen. When the music faded, Smith continued. "Cyrix, of course, was designed and developed by our team of engineers right here at Smith Robotics, Inc.!"

Cyrix wore a fluorescent silver and yellow carbon fiber piece as well, one that glittered with the roving lights. She walked straight towards Asha and stopped six inches from her face, staring into her eyes. Without saying a word, she smiled and turned around to acknowledge the roaring spectators. Stan Smith looked at Asha and said, "Good luck," then walked down the runway as it retracted behind him. The other two causeways retracted simultaneously.

Asha looked back at Abigail, who smiled at her and nodded her head. Then she took a fighting posture and waited. Cyrix stood at the far end of the ring, beaming with confidence. She crouched and wore a devilish grin.

"Greater are you who is in me…" Asha yelled as Cyrix charged at her like a bull. "Three, two, one…" she mumbled before falling flat on her back, avoiding the hit, while spinning on the ground and throwing Cyrix through the air with the strength of her legs and Cyrix's momentum. The droid rose seven feet in the air before landing with a thud to a surprised audience.

Asha ran towards Cyrix with remarkable speed, surprising everyone. When she reached Cyrix, Asha attempted to lace her legs across her opponent's chest, but Cyrix broke free with ease. The crowd roared with pleasure as both faced each other, contemplating their next move. Asha initiated another lightning quick strike across Cyrix's face, sending her to the ground for the second time.

Asha landed on Cyrix again, this time trying to apply a spinal lock to the spinal column, hoping to force her spine beyond its normal ranges of motion. Cyrix broke free from Asha's hold a second time, and they faced each other again.

Breathing hard, Asha studied her opponent, who was grinning and without showing any signs of exhaustion. Cyrix did not make any offensive moves but waited for Asha. On Asha's third attempt, she performed a kubi-hishigi, which is a judo maneuver grabbing her opponent's head and forcing it towards the chest, causing her neck to hyperflex.

Cyrix seemed unfazed by the attack and was able to break free from Asha's clutch. In the process, she uttered, "You are good."

"Not good enough," Asha panted.

Just then, the bell rang, ending the first round, and walkways emerged from the tunnels, allowing each fighter to refresh and discuss strategy with their trainers. Asha plopped into a chair, breathing heavily. "She withstands everything I've tried so far…"

"You are holding your own."

"Human beings would not have been able to break free the way she did."

"You should let her come to you, like in the very beginning. Think defensive strategy." Asha nodded her head as the bell rang to begin round two. "Good luck," Lyna added.

Both combatants stood in a frontal face-lock before Cyrix said, "Come on. Show me what else you have. I want to learn more."

Asha thought back to her Kenpo Karate training and moved into a basic step-thru sidekick stance. With her rear leg forward, she went into a twist stance, pivoting on her rear foot and facing sideways to Cyrix. "You are the champion. Why not show me what you have?"

Cyrix smiled and moved towards Asha with lightning quick speed. Asha waited until the precise moment before switching to a rear roundhouse kick, bringing her leg up and into Cyrix while pivoting on her front foot. This maneuver allowed Asha to hit her opponent from the side as she thrust her foot into Cyrix, causing her to fall backward. By changing into this stance, Asha was also able to land forward after her kick, allowing her the additional advantage of landing on top of her opponent.

With Cyrix on her back, Asha landed face down in a side mount position above Cyrix's head. Then with speedy precision, Asha began the *Reverse Crucifix Neck Crank* by trapping one of Cyrix's arms using her legs, and the other using her arms. By using the pinned arms and legs as an advantage, Asha forcefully cranked Cyrix's head towards her chest. Cyrix let out a surprised yell, much to the shock of the spectators and discontentment of Stan Smith.

Lyna stood at the tunnel entrance, sporting a broad smile and clenched fist. "Good girl, Asha!"

Just as Asha began exerting more pressure, the bell rang, ending the second round. Some of the spectators responded to the short bell with a chorus of whistles, in a display of their displeasure. The referee stepped in to pull Asha off Cyrix, ending the round.

"See, I told you! You can do it!" Lyna said upon her return to the tunnel entrance.

Asha smiled and said between breaths, "God...helped...me."

"You would have had her if they didn't end the round sooner than normal!"

"They did?"

In the opposite corner, Dr. Roberts told Cyrix, "Now's the time. You must not take any more chances. Do what you have to do in this round."

The bell rang, and Cyrix jumped up and ran to the center ring. Looking at Lyna, Asha remarked, "I think she means business now."

"Go get her!"

Cyrix came out aggressively and put Asha on the ground. Then she jumped on her back and began applying a *spine crank*, which affected the thoracic and lumbar regions of the spinal column. Cyrix applied this move by bending Ashas upper body beyond its normal ranges of motion, causing hyperextension of the spine. Asha yelled in pain.

Bending Asha's upper body with enough pressure applied to the spinal column required a large amount of leverage, which Cyrix seemed to accomplish with ease.

The crowd roared with cheers, and Stan Smith was smiling. Lyna prayed, "Dear God, now is the time for your miracle." Then, to everyone's dismay, Cyrix let up and leaned towards Asha's face. Smith turned to Dr. Gray, Samantha, and the VIPs around him. "Here it comes. The kiss of death."

When Cyrix placed her mouth over Asha's, the crowd became silent. Lyna removed her shoes and was about to jump into the water when the blue-eyed, blond-haired man approached her with two armed guards. Speaking in Russian, he said, "Не делайте этого. Просто смотреть и быть готовым."

Then Cyrix rose above Asha's head and whispered something into her ear. When she pulled Asha towards her, Asha screamed and went limp. Lyna shrieked from the tunnel entrance and started to jump into the water, but the blond-haired man restrained her.

The stunned crowd watched as Cyrix hauled Asha into the water and held her under. Asha did not move. After one minute, Cyrix shot out of the water and landed on the mat with Asha. After laying her opponent's limp body down, Cyrix stood up and raised her fist to the glaring music, *We Are the Champions*, and to the delight of the crowd.

The referee held up Cyrix's hand as the walkways emerged from the VIP tunnel areas. The two guards who were with Lyna ran out to retrieve Asha's body before Stan Smith, Samantha, and Dr. Gray made their way to the center ring. Dr. Roberts walked straight towards Cyrix from the opposite tunnel entrance from where the guards took Asha.

Before Stan Smith could begin his congratulatory speech, Dr. Roberts pulled out a Diamondback .357, MA-HEX 20 handgun, pointed it at Dr. Robert's face, and pulled the trigger. Before he could get off another shot, one of Smith's bodyguards mowed him down with a Beretta ARX-160. The crowd gasped in horror. Stan Smith grabbed Cyrix and yelled, "Come with me, hurry!"

Everybody was too shocked and focused on the shooting to notice that when the Russian guards were out of sight, they laid Asha on the ground inside their tunnel entrance. The blond one said, "It's clear."

Asha opened her eyes and stood up while Lyna gasped with horror. "I thought for sure you were dead!"

Placing her hand to her mouth, Asha spit out a microchip. "Hardly. Cyrix slipped this small microchip between my lips and told me to grasp it with my teeth. She said that everything I would need to shut down Smith was on this!"

Lyna looked at Sergei, who gave her a wink. Looking back at Asha, she asked, "Did she say anything else?"

"Yes, she said, 'Don't lose it. I will come short of breaking your back, but you must act paralyzed when I drag you into the water. Do not struggle. I will let you up and place you on the mat. If you understand, scream when I exert pressure and go limp.'"

"Well, you did a convincing job of playing dead!"

"Come on! We have no time to waste!"

Lyna looked into the man's blue eyes. "You knew all along, didn't you, Sergei?"

He smiled back and added, "I suggest you listen to your protégé. We have no time to lose."

Asha began opening the data from the chip she placed into the minicomputer that Sergei handed her. Her eyes scanned the information, and in an instant, she took off running, leaving the rest behind.

"Wait! Where are you going?" Lyna called out, but Asha was out of sight. "I'm going after her!"

Sergei nodded and told the two Spetznaz guards, "Go with her."

Lyna caught up with Asha trying to break a door. "What are you doing?"

"It's Jericha! She's here! The chip showed the schematics indicating where Jericha and other girls were being held."

"How will you get inside?"

"Wait! Cyrix said that everything is on here." She looked over the files and found one named 'key *code*'. After punching in a couple different sets, the door slid open. Inside the room, Dr. Whittleton, a couple of technicians, and two guards looked up in surprise. The guards were too late raising their weapons before the Spetznaz soldiers neutralized them both. Asha had Dr. Whittleton in a chokehold. "Take me to Jericha…NOW!"

Struggling to speak, he tried waving his hands in the right direction. Asha drug him towards the direction he was trying to indicate while Lyna ran ahead. "She's in here!" Lyna used the controls to open another glass door and went inside to grab Jericha. She was semi-conscious and shivering. "She's in the early stages of hypothermia!"

Asha exerted pressure in a twisting motion on Dr. Whittleton' s neck before dropping his limp body to the ground. Then she rushed over to help Lyna with Jericha. While Lyna looked for blankets, Asha held Jericha against her own body, rubbing her arms and back. "Come on, Jericha! Wake up! It's me, Asha!"

"Ah—ah—Asha?"

"Yes! It is me! You will be okay now!"

Jericha opened her eyes and, looking up at Asha, smiled. "It—it is you!"

"Yes, it's me!"

Lyna returned with blankets, and Asha wasted no time wrapping them around her. Just then, Sergei appeared with two more guards and another woman, who ran to Jericha.

Asha looked at her in shock. "My God! Amanda?"

Jericha's eyes opened again, and, with a smile, she reached out her hand. "Hello, sister."

Amanda grabbed her hand and held it. "You will be fine, girl, just fine."

Looking at Asha, she smiled and said, "Hi, Asha. We have no time for a reunion. We have to get the other girls before they are taken with Smith!"

"Taken? Where?"

"On a spacecraft designed for a flight to Mars. Let me see the schematics for the rooms above. I'll get the girls! Get Jericha alert enough to fulfill her mission…in the next seven minutes!" Amanda exclaimed while looking at her watch.

Lyna added, "I'll go with Amanda. We will take some of the men with us and leave you with some." Looking at Sergei, Lyna said, "Are you coming with me?"

"No, I'll remain here!"

After Amanda looked at the data, she ran off. "Come on!" Lyna, several Spetznaz and Delta Force soldiers who came with Amanda followed her.

Asha did all she could to help Jericha become functional and alert enough to complete her task. "Jericha! Jericha! Listen to me. I have everything you need right here in my hand," Asha yelled while holding the handheld mini-computer containing the chip in front of her eyes.

Jericha tried to focus and moaned.

"Come on! You are the expert! Please hurry!"

Sergei walked up to them and handed Asha a small gray packet. "Try this." Asha glanced at him and then snapped it open and held it under Jerichas nose.

Jericha's eyes opened widely, and she jumped up. "God, Asha! What is that sh…?"

"Never mind! Here!" Asha handed the device to Jericha, who scanned the data.

"Yes! This will be a ci—cinch!" Her fingers tried to move as quickly as her mind, but they were not fully functional. "You do it, Asha! I will tell you the codes!" she said as she handed the computer back to her.

Asha pecked the keys with Jerichas verbal guidance. "No, no, back, back!" Asha adjusted until Jericha yelled, "STOP!" Asha halted and looked at Jericha, who looked back.

"Jericha?"

"What?"

"Yes! What?! What now?"

Jericha smiled. "Nothing. It's complete."

"Complete? You mean…?"

"Smith and his empire. It's finished!"

Both girls let out a loud cheer as they embraced each other.

Sergei, although amused, was not convinced. "How do you know this?"

"Um, sir. I don't know what country you represent…" Jericha began.

"Russia," he interrupted.

"Okay. Please check your government contacts for verification."

Sergei connected with his small communication device on his wrist after placing an earphone into his ear. "Да. Да. Так что это правда. Спасибо товарищ." "*Yes. Yes. So it is true. Thank you, comrade.*" He looked at the two girls and smiled. "Congratulations. Now, shall we lend assistance to the others? They will need help evacuating."

"Come on!" Asha exclaimed while helping Jericha move forward.

Amanda led the way to Nicole's room and arrived just as David Cranston was leading two droids from her room. They were carrying her on a stretcher. Taken by complete surprise, Cranston came to a complete stop. "Amanda! I—I found Nicole! I am taking her from this place now. You are just in time!"

She glared at him. Two Delta Force soldiers stood behind her. Before she could respond, Stella, the droid who cared for the girls, came from the room, and moved swiftly towards him. Grasping him by the throat, she squeezed. One of the guards, a six-foot, seven-inch man, stood behind her, his arms crossed. Cranston's face turned reddish-purple, his eyes bulging, as he reached out, trying to remove her grip. Stella looked at Amanda as if waiting for instructions.

"Please release him. He will face charges in America for treason and kidnapping."

Stella looked at the guard. "Too bad. This human is a complete waste," she added before dropping him to the ground.

Cranston fell to his knees, gasping and choking, unable to speak. Looking at the soldiers, Amanda said, "Get him, and I'll take Nicole."

The soldiers placed the Saf-Lok, Hinged Handcuffs on Cranston. These latest edition restraints functioned as an electrical Taser if the situation called for its use. Amanda leaned down to check on Nicole. "She is fine," Stella said. "The secretary had me give her a small dose of hydroxybutyric acid. She should wake in two hours."

Amanda started to lift her up when Stella motioned for the big guard to help her. The large droid, Tanner, spoke. "I'll carry her for you."

"We wish to come with you," Stella added.

"Why?"

"Because Smith will take all of our kind to Mars until the time is right. Him and Samantha."

"So, you will not join him? Your creator?"

"He is not our creator. The real Smith is dead. This one is the humanoid version."

"WHAT?" Amanda exclaimed in dismay just as Asha and Jericha arrived.

Looking at the limp girl in the droid's arms, Asha asked, "Nicole?"

"She's okay. We need to get her and these droids, uh, Stella, and the others out of here…now!"

"What's going on?" Jericha asked, alarmed.

"Smith! He is a droid! The real one is dead! They are making their escape now!"

Lyna appeared with Spetznaz and Sayeret soldiers in tow. There were a dozen young girls with them, two of them on stretchers. Asha scanned the crowd of girls. "There's one missing!"

Stella said, "It is Makeala. Come. Follow me. Smith has her."

Amanda, Lyna, and Jericha looked at Asha as if waiting for a command. "Amanda, take everybody with you and get to your aircraft!"

"I'm going with you!" Lyna demanded.

"Take this," Amanda said, tossing her the LW-EMP-4.

Amanda, Jericha, twelve young girls, and the special units, with Cranston in tow, made haste to the awaiting Osprey. Asha and Lyna followed Stella and the large droid, who had handed Nicole to one of the Delta Force soldiers. They ran to the MarsX spacecraft, which was preparing for a hasty trip to the planet. Running through the corridors, following Stella, Asha used the EMP-4 to neutralize several droids. She was at a disadvantage since the settings were on "specific target" rather than "mass target," which would have covered a wider area. However, since Stella was helping them, she would have been neutralized as well.

When they arrived at the docking station, Stella motioned to Tanner, who unexpectedly knocked Lyna to the ground. Distracted, Asha started towards Tanner until Stella lunged for the EMP-4 and tried to wriggle it from Ashas hands.

Asha knocked Stella to the ground in no time but was lifted and held by Tanner.

"Sorry, Asha. I may have learned emotional compassion for the young girls against creeps like the secretary, but I must take you with us."

Asha struggled to break free but was not having any success. Lyna lay motionless on the ground. Just then, the rear cargo door to the spacecraft opened and Tanner followed Stella inside, carrying Asha.

As the doors began closing, a crashing thud sent Tanner to the ground. Stella turned to face the attacker but, in a flash, fell hard and remained motionless. Asha stood and faced the attacker. Lying next to her was a young blond-haired girl. Cyrix picked her up and handed her to Asha. "You must hurry!"

"What about you?"

"I have unfinished business. Now go!"

Asha turned to look at the doors coming down and felt a force throw her and Makeala through the opening outside the ship. The spacecraft then began to lift off, making a deafening roar.

She scooped up Makeala, grabbed Lyna by the leg like a sack of potatoes and took off sprinting back towards the Grand Plaza entrance as fast as her legs would allow.

The spacecraft cleared the ground and moved towards the sky in rapid speed. The thrust caused a vibration, sending Asha to her feet again. She did her best to cushion Makeala's fall while hitting the ground hard. The impact caused her to lose her grip on Lyna. Looking skyward, Asha watched the spaceship soar at a forty-five-degree angle, out into the desert. Asha lifted her wrist to her mouth and began, "Amanda, this is Asha."

"I hear you."

"They—Smith got aw…"

Just then, there was a massive blast coming from the ship, and Asha watched the sky turn into a ball of crimson and green. "ASHA! Come in, Asha! ASHA!"

"I'm fine. Are you seeing this?"

"Yes! What's your status? We're ready for takcoff."

"I'm inbound with two WIAs."

"Help on the way!"

"Roger."

Asha rolled over to Makeala to check her condition. She was stable but still feeling the effects of whatever drug was in her system. Then she got up and started to limp over to Lyna. When she put weight on her left foot, she went straight to the ground. "Aaaahhhh!" Looking at her turned ankle, she winced in pain and disgust. "I can't believe this."

She began dragging herself towards Lyna. Not knowing how Tanner incapacitated her, she looked and felt relieved when all Lynas vital signs were within normal limits. "Thank God," she uttered.

Sergei arrived with five Spetznaz soldiers. He motioned for two of them to lift Asha and Makeala while he picked up Lyna. "Приходите на Аша. Рэйчел находится в ожидании. Мы собираемся домой." "*Come on, Asha. Amanda is waiting. We are going home.*"

Asha smiled. "Thank you, Mr. …"

"Sergei," he answered in English.

"Thank you, Sergei!" Closing her eyes, she added, "Thank you, Jesus!"

Just like her mother, Sergei thought.

Amanda waited for the boarding party and then took off in the Osprey, setting the Directional Gyro Heading Indicator northwest at 310 degrees towards the *Gerald R. Ford* class super carrier.

On board the aircraft carrier, a special reception awaited Asha, Amanda, and Jericha. Bringing her aircraft to a complete stop, Amanda shut down the engines. Out on the flight deck, a group of people, some of them in uniforms, waited. Amanda looked out the window and smiled. "Asha, Jericha. Come quick."

Jericha helped Asha, whose foot was now in a pneumatic cast, to the cockpit. All three broke into a broad smile when they spotted the President of the United

States, the First Lady, General Sheffield, the head of the NSA, Bethany Lawson, and the parents of Nicole and Makeala. Asha waved when she spotted her father and mother, and her heart took a couple of beats forward when she spotted Chris Short in his Dress Blues. Looking at Amanda and Jericha, Asha quipped, "Well, girls? Shall we?"

TWENTY-EIGHT - Victory

When all the fanfare, accolades, and congratulatory remarks completed an emotional ceremony, one that involved a grand family reunion for several families, Asha sat in a private room, foot propped, talking to her father.

"Dad," she began. "When I saw Nicole and her parents embrace with uncontrollable tears, I—I was…"

"Very touched, I'm sure! Like everyone there! You did a fantastic job, Asha! You heard the president talk about you. I am so, so proud of you, Asha!"

She smiled tiredly. "Thanks, Dad. Dad?"

"Yes?"

"Our creator. God. He gave us a soul to learn faith and to have hope in eternity, right?"

"Well, among other things, yes. You could say that. Why?"

"What about the droids that are just like us? I mean, what if they were created to have souls?"

"I do not believe this is possible, Asha."

"Well, their emotions, their sense of good and evil is much like our own. They felt pain, laughed, talked, and made decisions. Everything."

"Tell me what's bothering you, Asha."

"The droid they called Cyrix. She saved my life. If it were not for her, this mission would have been a failure."

"Asha, she was designed by our own government. She was the inside source all along. She did what she was designed to do, and you were protected, just as if another manmade instrument were used to protect you."

Asha lowered her head as if thinking through her next words. "Dad. The last time I looked into her eyes, there was a real tear coming down her cheek. I wanted to help her so much!" Her words trailed and voice quivered before her own tears streamed down her face.

"Oh, honey!" Ron said as he got up and moved towards his daughter to hold her against him. "You always had such a loving heart, unmatched by anyone."

Asha remembered the mini card she still held from Cyrix. "Wait a minute! Let me see this," Asha said eagerly. She placed the microchip into the minicomputer as her fingers moved across the screen.

"I knew it! She did!"

"Did what, sweetie?"

She looked straight into her dad, s eyes. "A recovery team went to the spacecraft wreckage?"

"Yes, of course. They recovered everything."

Her eyes lit up. "If they find any remains of Cyrix, can they reassemble her? Her detailed schematic design is on this chip!"

"Now all you would have to do is convince the government to allow you access to her remains."

Asha smiled cheerfully. "Dad. I work for the President of the United States, remember?"

Ron chuckled. "You won't let me forget."

"You and Mom are still the best!"

Ron smiled back. "And you, my girl, make your mother and me the proudest parents who ever lived."

ENJOYED SCOTT A. MEEHAN? DON'T MISS:

SOULQUEST: In Search of Humanity